WREATHS
OF
GLORY

A WESTERN STORY

WREATHS
OF
GLORY

A WESTERN STORY

JOHNNY D. BOGGS

Copyright © 2013 by Johnny D. Boggs
Published in 2017 by Blackstone Publishing
Cover design by Alenka Vdovič Linaschke

Printed in the United States of America

ISBN 978-1-4708-6153-7

1 3 5 7 9 10 8 6 4 2

CIP data for this book is available
from the Library of Congress

Blackstone Publishing
31 Mistletoe Rd.
Ashland, OR 97520

www.BlackstonePublishing.com

For the Rountree Family,
Russ, Katie, Chelsea, and Ben

"True, they tell us wreaths of glory,
Evermore will deck his brow,
But this soothes the anguish only,
Sweeping o'er our heartstrings now."

From "The Vacant Chair", 1861
Lyrics by Henry S. Washburn. Music by George F. Root

MISSOURI

CHAPTER ONE

Alistair Durant came down with a mighty bad case of bowel complaint two days before the Battle of Wilson's Creek, which explains why he didn't get to shoot any Yankees, how come he got captured, and the reason he found himself walking back to Clay County two weeks later with a parole in his pocket.

"Hotter than the hinges of Hades," Alistair's pa would have told him—if, that is, Able Gideon Durant were still speaking to him—but that was to be expected. Late August. Missouri. "In this part of the country, these dog days could singe Lucifer's horns, and melt his pitchfork." That was another of Pa's sayings.

Now, why in thunderation do I keep thinking about Pa? Alistair said to himself, and found a shady spot underneath some oaks to study on that. Of course, he already knew the answer. Nothing perplexing about it at all. He just needed an excuse, is all, to get out of that sun, rest a spell, slake his thirst, and put off the inevitable, even though he had a long walk ahead of him before he ever reached home.

Removing his battered slouch hat, he ran long fingers through wet brown hair, then found the canteen slung over his shoulder, about the only thing the Yanks let him keep. They had robbed him of what little money he carried, even took his venison jerky. Worst of all, they had taken his shotgun. Pa would raise Cain about losing that old 12-gauge. Then again, as tight as Pa appeared to be with bluebellies, maybe he could arrange to have that double-barrel returned. Alistair pulled out the canteen's cork, sloshed around the liquid, thinking that might cool off the water a mite, at least make it taste better.

It didn't. Brackish and like to be boiling hot. Still, it seemed to cool once it traveled down his throat, and the shade certainly comforted him. He started to stretch out his long legs, but crossed the left instead, removed his brogan, and rubbed his foot. He didn't have any socks, and both feet felt blisters coming along.

How far is it home? he asked himself, recrossed his legs, and began massaging his right foot.

Nigh two hundred miles, a Yankee corporal had told him before sending him along with that parole. Criminy, before joining the Missouri State Guard, other than that one trip to Independence Pa had let him come on three years back, Alistair figured that he had never seen anything of Missouri other than Centerville, his farm, and Watkins Mill. On the other hand, Greene County didn't look a whole lot different than Clay County. Certainly not any better.

"If I'm still in Greene County," he said aloud, and began shoving a small, worn brogan back on his still-aching foot.

"You ain't."

The voice startled Alistair right off the stump he was using as a chair. Jumping up, spilling water on the front of his trousers so that it looked as if he'd just peed his pants, he dropped his hat and left shoe, and kicked off his right, and stared at a gangling boy with the greenest eyes Alistair had ever seen.

The long-haired kid laughed, shaking his head and saying: "Didn't mean to give you such a fright, fella."

Oh, he had meant that, though. Alistair could tell. "You didn't." Alistair tried to dry his britches, but gave up, sat down, and began collecting brogans and hat.

"Pole," the tall boy said.

Alistair stared. Blinked. Finally said: "My name's Durant. Alistair Durant. Glad to meet you, Pole." He wasn't, of course.

The kid laughed again, almost doubled over, and slapped his thighs. "No. No. My name ain't Pole. We's in Pole County. That's what I was sayin'. 'Bout five miles back, I met a gent on a mule, ridin' south he was, and he tells me that Bolivar be ten miles up this road. Says it's the county seat of Pole County. That Pole County was named after one of our Presidents, but I disremember that President's first name."

Alistair corked his canteen, returned it over his shoulder, and studied on what he thought he had just heard.

"Well ..." The tall boy had done some mental work himself. "No. Ain't our country no more. What I meant to say was that Pole County's named after one of the Presidents of the United States, but not that Abolitionist, Southern-hatin' Lincoln." He punctuated that with a firm nod.

"Name's Beans Kimbrough." He offered a bony right hand.

Alistair shook it. Then said: "There's never been a president named Pole, United States or Confederate."

"Well, it be somethin' like that."

"Polk," Alistair said. "James A. Polk."

"Poke. Right funny name for a politician."

"Polk." He had to enunciate.

Beans Kimbrough, however, had already lost interest. He pulled a flask from his trousers pocket, unscrewed the lid, and took a pull, smacking his lips. He offered the fancy-engraved pewter container to Alistair, who shook his head.

"Corn liquor," Beans said. "Aged thirty days. So the man on the mule told me. Traded him a plug of 'baccy for it."

"No," Alistair said. "Still off my feed. Stomach's not ready for any liquor."

"You get shot in the belly?" Beans asked.

"No." Alistair swallowed, and suddenly felt chilled. He remembered those boys and old men. Gut-shot. Baking in the broiling sun. Yankee sawbones wouldn't even try to help them, or make them comfortable. Just left them outside baking in the sun. To die. Beans sat beside Alistair, took another swallow, then began rubbing his own feet. He was barefoot, and that got Alistair thinking. So he pulled off his brogans, and chucked them into the woods. Keep wearing those heavy things, and he'd be crippled long before he ever set foot in Clay County.

"You comin' up from Springfield way, Alice?"

"Alistair," he corrected, feeling his face flush before deciding that Beans hadn't meant any insult. He was just dumb as the rotting stump they were sitting on.

"Kill any Yanks?"

"Never got a chance to even fire a gun," Alistair said.

"I did," Beans said. "I mean, fire my musket."

That impressed Alistair. He recalled the din of battle all around him. Like the worst thunderstorm in the annals of Missouri history. Lying atop his blanket, he could feel the earth tremble from cannon and musketry, the pounding of horses' hoofs, the rumble of caisson and wagons. Remembered his own torn feelings—wishing he were taking part in that fighting, but at the same time relieved that he was in the hospital field, safe.

Later, he'd wish he were anywhere but there—after the Federals had taken him and the other sick soldiers prisoner, once the wounded soldiers began being carted back. And the dead. He would have given anything short of his soul to be away from those horrible screams, the sickening smell of blood, and the ruined arms and legs being tossed out of the surgeon's tent, into a wheelbarrow like garbage.

He shut his mind to those images—him lying sick with the trots while arms and legs were being sawed off boys Northern and Southern—and tried to focus on what all Beans Kimbrough was saying.

Something didn't register, and, brow knotted, Alistair looked at the newcomer, asking: "Could you repeat that?"

Beans stared at him as if he were an oaf. "I said," Beans told him, slowing his already molasses drawl, "but ... I ... didn't ... shoot ... at ... no ... bluebelly." His usual cadence returned. "Drew me a bead on that no-account Sergeant McGarrity is what I done."

Beans picked up his flask, took another sip, and absently passed it to Alistair. This time, Alistair accepted it.

The liquor went down like coal oil, even though Alistair had taken just a wee taste. He felt he might gag when that whiskey exploded in his belly, but his bowels didn't loosen, nothing climbed up his throat except a slight cough, and he returned the flask to Beans Kimbrough.

"Had him dead to rights, till, Hans Hagen, the sorry little Hun, calls out ... 'Look out, Sergeant, he aims to murder you!'" Beans said. "And McGarrity, lucky Irishman that he is, ducked, and all my ball did was knock off his bummer cap. So I decided I'd best foot it out of there. Dropped that musket, and run, I did. Hid in the woods, till the Yanks retreated back to Springfield and other parts. Till I heared that Price was takin' our boys off toward Fort Scott. Figured they wasn't gonna spare no soldiers to come lookin' for me, so I decided to walk back home. Reckon I'm through with this war."

"Me, too," Alistair said, the forty-rod already loosening his tongue.

"Well," Beans said. "I'm through with the Missouri State Guard, anyhows."

Suddenly what Beans Kimbrough had been saying, confessing, whatever you wanted to call it, registered with Alistair Durant.

"You mean ...?" He had to swallow to get his voice back. "You mean you shot at your own sergeant?"

"Shot to kill." Beans Kimbrough's head bobbed with pride. "I warrant that Irishman was a Yankee spy. Tryin' to torment all us boys in the guard."

"That's …" Alistair stopped. He was about to say crazy, but Beans Kimbrough was staring at him, their faces so close Alistair could see the hairs of Beans' peach-fuzz mustache, and his green eyes had turned colder than February sleet.

"You quit, too?" Beans asked.

"You mean desert?" Again, Alistair took the flask, swallowed another sip, and coughed, shaking his head, feeling his eyes water.

"Not desert. I mean quit that fool army? Ain't no way to fight no war, I tell you that. Sergeants tellin' you to stand this way, walk this way, shoot when they tells you to shoot. Fancy paradin'. Follow orders like that, and you'll wind up deader than that Federal general named Lyons us Rebs kilt." Beans polished off the rest of the liquor, and slid the empty flask into his pocket as he stood.

"So, you quit?" Beans asked.

Alistair shook his head. "No, I got captured."

"You don't say!" Beans extended his hand, and Alistair realized he meant to help him to his feet. He accepted, and that bony hand of Beans Kimbrough felt like a vise. "Then you escaped, eh?"

His head shook, but he said nothing.

"Well, then how come you're out on this road?" Beans stared suspiciously down the road to Springfield, and into the woods. "Why ain't you marchin' to Kansas with Gen'ral Price?"

"They paroled me."

Beans grinned. "You joshin'?"

Alistair started to show Beans the parole paper, but decided that wasn't necessary.

"Mean to tell me them bluebellies just turned you loose?" Beans asked.

His nod seemed shaky.

"So, let me ask you again. How come you ain't trottin' after Gen'ral Price?"

"Can't. Swore not to take up arms against the Union."

"Huh?" Beans shook his head. "Dumbest thing I ever heard.

Yankees ain't no smarter than Confederates. Where you bound, Alvin?"

"A-li-stair."

"Alistair." Beans said it slowly, then repeated the name. "Funny name."

"'Beans' ain't exactly 'John'." The corn whiskey had affected him, Alistair knew. Ma would have a cow if she heard him say *ain't*, though she used it all the time.

That got Beans Kimbrough hooting like a stuttering owl. That pinching right hand clamped on Alistair's left shoulder, until it felt like that tall deserter would break his collar bone. "That's right funny, Al-i-stair." Beans finally released his grip to push back his straw hat. "I like you, Ally—I done forgot your last name."

"Durant."

"Where you from?"

"Northeast of Centerville. That's up in Clay County."

"I know."

"You heard of it?" Alistair couldn't disguise his surprise. Beans Kimbrough didn't even know President Polk's name, yet he had heard of Centerville, which never impressed Alistair as much of a town, and Clay County, which was populated by—his father one prime exception—mostly slave-owning, Kentucky Baptists who had been preaching Secession long before this war had started.

"Heard of it, even been there. I got an uncle at Blue Springs. That's over in Jackson County, east of Independence. So I'd pay him a visit time to time … well, Pa'd send me there to work. Last summer, Uncle Morgan said I wasn't no use to him on the plantation, so he practically indentured me to old man Watkins. Had to start cardin' wool. That'll age you. Imagine bein' cooped up in a furnace. Ten times hotter than this."

"They just opened that mill last year," Alistair said.

"Wished they'd closed it a day later."

"You going back to the mill?"

"Not hardly."

"Independence?"

"Nah. Reckon I wore out my welcome with Uncle Morgan. So I'm walkin' home."

"Where's that?"

Beans gestured. "Osceola. Want some company?" Expecting to be denied, Beans went on. "Osceola's only thirty, forty miles north of Bolivar, and I warrant we're only three, four miles from that town. But then you got another hundred miles or so to Independence from Bolivar. And Centerville's a good day's walk from Independence, though I reckon you could probably find some farmer to let you ride in his wagon. But I warrant my folks would feed you, and if there's a bunch of State Guard boys hangin' 'round the farm, lookin' for me, might could be I'd join you. Got no hankerin' to see the Guard no more. Had my fill of bein' hung up by my thumbs."

"Sure. I'd enjoy the company."

Beans stared at Alistair's feet, then looked over at the trunk of an elm. "You ain't gonna wear them shoes?"

"Hurt too bad. Too small, I think."

The tall boy looked again at Alistair's feet. "Well, sir, if they don't fit you, they sure ain't gonna fit me. Might as well start walkin'."

Later Alistair Durant would wonder what would have happened had he declined the offer, and stuck around in the shade to rub his feet some more.

The boy from Osceola was already heading toward the road, and as tall as he was, as fast as he walked, Alistair regretted agreeing to join him, even if only as far as Osceola. He hurried to catch up.

CHAPTER TWO

By evening, they had made it about six miles north of Bolivar, having stopped in that burg just long enough to refill their canteens and Beans' flask, all with water from the well on the square. Good water it was, too, cool and refreshing, and not salty or hard as if it had been cured with a rusty horseshoe. Worn to a frazzle, they made camp on the banks of a pond that drained off some branch. Beans had guessed that they might catch a fish for supper. Alistair had argued that it was too hot for the fish to bite, even after the sun set.

"Only thing we'll catch here"—Alistair had slapped at a mosquito—"is yellow fever."

Now, huddled by a fire made from green wood for smoke to keep those bloodsuckers away, Beans Kimbrough agreed that Alistair had been right.

Next, Beans asked: "Got anything to eat?"

Alistair shook his head sadly. His stomach echoed the rumbling in Beans' belly. "Not even jerky." Silently he damned those thieving Yankees who had captured him.

With a sigh, Beans leaned closer to the fire, into smoke that seemed to follow Beans, and away from Alistair, who killed another mosquito. "Reckon we shoulda taken our sup back in Bolivar."

"With what?" Alistair snapped, his hunger shortening his patience and the usually long fuse to his temper. "Yankees stole what little money I had."

"Well, I coulda traded my flask for some crackers and cheese." Beans leaned back, and grinned wickedly. "Or they's other ways of gettin' grub."

Muttering an oath, Alistair moved around the fire, and forced his way onto the stump where Beans sat, letting the smoke envelope him and relieve him from pesky bugs. For once, the smoke didn't move away from him, perhaps, he thought, because it seemed to think Beans Kimbrough was a chimney. Tall enough for one, Alistair conceded.

"We passed that farm about a quarter mile back," Alistair said. When Beans didn't comment, he continued. "Well, his corn crop looked good. Doubt if he'd begrudge us a few ears."

"Raw corn ain't appetizin'. Druther have ham and eggs."

"I ain't stealing a pig, and I ain't raiding a chicken coop." He shook his head in exasperation, not only for his companion's lack of morals, but the fact that *ain't* was entering his vocabulary after one afternoon with Beans Kimbrough. "Good way to get shot."

Beans shrugged. "Reckon we could roast 'em ears." He opened his mouth to speak again—maybe, Alistair hoped, to volunteer to fetch the corn so Alistair could have the smoke and stump to himself—but the sound of hoofs on the road stopped him, and he was unbuttoning his blouse, his right hand gripping the butt of a small revolver.

The horse had stopped. Above the crackling of the fire, Alistair heard the creaking of saddle leather, but he didn't look at the road. His eyes fixated on the revolver, and his mouth dropped open. He had not known that Beans was armed.

Beans pulled the revolver, squatting now, but backing deeper into the thicket, whispering: "You stay here. I'll cover you iffen he comes."

Alistair wanted to protest, but couldn't find his voice. He could hear Beans' bare feet trudging through the mud, then a voice called from the road: "Hello, the camp!"

"Uh." Alistair swallowed, inhaled deeply, and blew out air from his mouth. "Yeah?" he called out.

"Might I come in? I am alone. Mean you no harm. But coffee would hit the spot."

He found himself looking all around, expecting the woods to be filled with Confederate provosts hunting down Beans Kimbrough. His companion had tried to murder a sergeant. Certainly the Confederate Army would go hard on anyone traveling with a scalawag like that, even if Alistair did have a parole paper signed by some Yankee officer.

"We ain't got …" He sighed, swallowed, tried again. "I don't have any coffee." *Nothing but smoke and skeeters*, he thought bitterly.

"I do."

Alistair blinked.

"Bacon, too. And six ears of sweet corn."

Behind Alistair came the metallic click of Beans Kimbrough's pea-shooter pistol. "Invite him in," Beans whispered.

"Well …" Alistair licked his lips. He wanted to warn this wayfarer to keep on riding, that if he came into this camp he might wind up dead, but the stranger had already dismounted and was leading his horse off the road, and into the clearing.

"I mean you lads no harm," the man said. With the fire in front of him and smoke burning his eyes, Alistair couldn't really see the man, but he could hear just fine. *Lads*, he had said. Plural. "Either of you," the stranger continued. "You at the fire. And you in the mud with a revolver." He wrapped the reins around a bush, and stepped closer to the fire, extending his hands as if to warm himself.

Slowly Alistair rose.

The stranger smiled. He cut quite the figure. An inch or two taller than Alistair, but well short of matching Beans Kimbrough's height. Sandy hair, a plumed hat set at a rakish angle. Waxed mustache. Eyes a brilliant blue, with lids that drooped and made him look serious or sad, Alistair couldn't quite make up his mind as to which. His unbuttoned jacket was gray, with yellow French braids stitched onto the sleeves. Tan trousers stuck inside black boots. And slipped inside a yellow sash was a brace of pistols, the ivory grips reflecting the flames of the fire.

"The coffee and grub are in my saddlebags," he said. "I even have the necessaries for cooking. If you will accept my company this evening. I thought I might continue on north, but since the weather remains hot, and I have ridden far already, and alone, I decided company would be delightful. I also have a volume of Shakespeare. I can read for my meals."

He had an easy way to make you relax. Spoke like a schoolteacher.

"Seems we should be reading to you," Alistair said. "You providing the food and all."

The man slapped his palms together, and laughed. "Then I choose *Hamlet*." He looked over Alistair's shoulder, into the woods, and Alistair knew he sought out Beans. "Shall I gather the food? Or keep riding?"

"Fetch the chow." Beans Kimbrough stepped out of the dark.

The man slapped his hands again, and returned to his fine black mare while Beans moved beside Alistair, slipping the little Colt into his pocket. When the stranger returned with the saddlebags and a canvas sack, Beans straightened, and his hand gripped the weapon's butt.

"My name," the newcomer said, "is Charley Hart."

The gun reappeared in Beans' hand. "Funny," he said, "I recollect it as Wilson Cantrell." He pulled the hammer back to full cock, and pointed the barrel over the fire and into the mustached man's face.

The stranger was a cool one. Alistair had to give him that. All he did was grin. "Quantrill, actually," the man said. "And William, not Wilson." Ignoring the pistol, he lowered the saddlebags, and squatted, opening one, retrieving coffee, small pot, and two cups. They'd have to share. Next, he dumped the corn from the canvas sack and opened the other leather pouch, pulling out a wrapped slab of bacon and a skillet. "'What's in a name? That which we call a rose by any other name would smell as sweet.'"

"*Romeo and Juliet*," Alistair heard himself saying.

Quantrill or Charley Hart, whoever he was, looked up from unwrapping the bacon, those eyes sparkling in appreciation, before he finally turned his attention to Beans Kimbrough, who hadn't lowered the revolver or eased off the trigger. "You have me at a disadvantage, young man. You know me, by any of my names, but I cannot quite place your face. Which, trust me, is rare for me."

"Last December. I was at my Uncle Morgan's plantation when you come by."

The sandy-haired man nodded at the memory, drew a knife from a sheath hidden somewhere on his back, and began carving thick slices of bacon. "Then you know," Quantrill said without looking up, "that I saved your uncle's property and his life."

"There are those," Beans shot back out, "that figured maybe we shoulda hung you."

"'Hanged' is the correct usage, young man." He dropped the slices into the skillet. "Let us not mince words, gentlemen. Do I take my bacon, coffee, and corn elsewhere, and, perchance, find a more hospitable pair with whom to pass the evening? Do I share it with you? Or do you, sir …?" His eyes were icy as he stared up past the short-barreled revolver into Beans Kimbrough's face. "Do you murder me and take my horse, food, and plunder?"

"Beans," Alistair said softly. Trying not to sound like he was pleading, though that's exactly what he was doing.

Hearing the click as Beans lowered the hammer, Alistair felt a weight removed off his tight shoulders. Beans started to return the revolver, but changed his mind, and kept it in his right hand. "I ain't et in a while," he said as he found his place on the stump. "Mayhap I'll shoot you after we've et."

Quantrill laughed heartily, and returned to fixing supper.

* * * * *

The way William Quantrill and Beans Kimbrough retold the story over coffee, corn, and bacon, things had happened something like this.

December last, a few weeks before Christmas, Beans had been eating dinner at his cousin's house when Quantrill knocked on the door. Andrew Walker lived about a quarter mile from his pa's. Quantrill must have mistaken the home for Morgan Walker's place.

"So he tells Andrew and me that he's come with a bunch of jayhawkers to rob Uncle Morgan and free all his slaves." Beans swallowed bacon, and bit into an ear of corn. "Says it like he's readin' from some newspaper. Bold as brass. I thought Andrew was gonna fetch his flintlock off the wall and blow your brains out."

With a grin, Quantrill shook his head. "Till you heard my plan." He stretched back, leaning his head against the saddle, rolling an ear of corn in his fingers.

"His plan was he goes back with his Kansans, comes back that night, but by then we've set up an ambuscade. All we got to do is shoot the devil out of jayhawkers."

"Sounds like a good plan," Alistair said, just to say something.

"It worked." Beans bit into the corn again. "Andrew rounded up some neighbors, we loaded our shotguns with buckshot, and Uncle Morgan comes home late that eve. Just maybe, I don't know, ten, twenty minutes before 'em thievin' jayhawkers arrive."

The ambush worked. The jayhawkers even brought a wagon to cart those slaves back to Kansas. Didn't expect anything till Quantrill, making a beeline for the door, dropped to his belly. Shotgun blasts shattered the stillness, and one Kansan fell dead. Two others were wounded, one of them managing to crawl into the wagon, which took off down the road. Another jayhawker helped the remaining wounded thief out of the yard, and they disappeared in the woods.

"What happened?" Alistair asked.

Beans looked at Quantrill, but the man merely waved his cob at Beans, like he was a schoolteacher choosing a student with pencil or ruler to answer a question.

"Waited till first light, then taken after the two afoot. One of Uncle Morgan's slaves found 'em hidin' in the brush, and they promised him his freedom if he could steal 'em a wagon and get 'em back to Lawrence. Instead, the darky come to us. And we went to rid us of some jayhawkers."

"You weren't there," Quantrill said softly. "I remember that much."

"No, sir. I wasn't. So maybe you could retell the story? Since you *was* there."

"The two jayhawkers were killed. Justice is swift." Quantrill pitched the cob toward the pond, but no splash sounded.

"I hear that Uncle Morgan killed one," Beans said. "Then you run up to the injured one, sticks your pistol in the poor guy's mouth, and blowed his head off." Likewise, Beans flung his ear into the darkness, and it splashed in the water, silencing croaking frogs for a moment. "Like you wanted to shut him up forever."

"I've heard the same story, young man." Quantrill pushed himself to a seated position. "But you weren't there. I was. No, your father killed one of the Kansans, and your cousin dispatched the other. But only because they were quicker than I. Still, I was satisfied. They were the last."

Silence fell like an avalanche. Seconds later, bullfrogs resumed their serenade. Alistair wiped kernels from his face, rubbed his hands on his trousers. "Last of what?" he asked.

This story William Quantrill told without interruption. Thirty jayhawkers had stopped Quantrill and his brother on the Kansas plains earlier. The brutes robbed them, but that wasn't all. They shot Quantrill in his chest and leg, then left him to die. He had been lucky. His brother had been tortured, screaming for death long before one of the Lawrence fiends found mercy enough to send a .44-caliber ball into the poor soul's brain.

Here, Quantrill paused long enough to retrieve a silk handkerchief from his breast pocket, and dab his eyes. "I felt blame. Shame. We should have stayed in Kentucky. Now, my brother ... poor, brave

Thomas Henry ... lay dead. I longed to join him, but resolve slowed the flow of blood. Saved my life. Nay, I recovered. Wound up in Lawrence. And joined the jayhawkers. To exact my own revenge."

Eighteen of the barbarians had been killed by Quantrill's own hand. It had taken months, luck, duplicity, the will of God. Yet no Kansan suspected Quantrill. The last to die had been those at Morgan Walker's plantation.

"Criminy," Alistair said.

For the longest time, William Quantrill stared into the flickering flames. At last he looked up, tears welling in his eyes. He smiled weakly at Alistair, and eventually made himself look at Beans.

"My pa always said your story stank like a bucket full of shit."

Quantrill grinned wickedly. He slapped his thigh. "I must meet your father, young man. He has a singular wit. Was he in the ambush of those rapscallions, too?"

"Nah. He don't do nothin' to risk his neck. Runs a store in Osceola. Hides behind the counter all day."

"But you are men of action." It wasn't a question. Alistair straightened, then thought about all the action he had seen. Sitting on a chamber pot while brave Missouri lads died. "As was Morgan Walker." He gestured toward the black mare. "If you remember everything, son," Quantrill told Beans, "your uncle presented me the following morning with Black Bess. And a saddle, bridle, new suit of clothes, and fifty dollars. Other fine Southern men of Independence added to the reward, though I sought nothing but to avenge my brother's death. Morgan Walker believed me. And his plantation near Blue Springs is where I am bound."

Beans stared at their guest with suspicion. "What for you goin' back there?"

"Sterling Price won a great battle for the South," Quantrill said, "but this war is not over. It has barely begun. General Lyons may be dead, but we must send others to hell after him. And mark my words, lads, there are many others. Fiends as wicked as that crazed demon

John Brown now burning in eternal damnation, thank the heavens. Men like Lane. Others we must fear. Others we must strike dead. Jayhawkers will continue to raid Missouri. Thusly I seek to recruit an army of brave Missourians who believe in the righteous cause of the South, the Confederacy. We will fight them on our terms, our way."

He stared first at Beans, then at Alistair. Like he wanted them to join up right then and there. When they didn't, Quantrill leaned back on his saddle, and smiled. "You think I am mad." He snorted. "Not that I blame you. But you have yet to see madness." His voice fell into a whisper. "You have yet to see madness."

CHAPTER THREE

"Well, now," said the tall boy leaning against the ivy-covered brick wall, "my prodigal brother has returned home."

"Hello, Darius." Beans Kimbrough spoke without any emotion at all. He half turned, giving a slight gesture toward Quantrill and Alistair, and introduced his companions. "I promised them some food."

Darius' grin lacked any mirth. He must have been four or five years younger than Beans, but had to be as tall as Alistair. "No fatted calf, Benedict."

Hard to figure. Now, Alistair had no brothers—he was the middle kid, two older sisters (though one, married and living up in St. Joseph, had died in childbirth three years back), and two younger twin sisters who needled him incessantly. He wouldn't say he was close to any of them, but he sure loved them, and would have expected a hug from all three had he just returned from war. Darius didn't seem pleased at all to see Beans. Beans didn't care one way or the other. So Alistair stared at the red-brick house.

That surprised him, too. So much, in fact, that Alistair felt shamed. He had figured Beans Kimbrough—even his given name, Benedict, didn't seem to fit—lived in some white trash shanty. Yet this two-story brick house stood in a neighborhood full of impressive structures. Three large windows, all open to catch the breeze, on the front of the upper story, two on the lower, fireplaces on both sides. Round white columns on the small porch. Ivy. Shade trees. A gazebo next to a raised flower garden in the front yard, and a swing hanging from the limbs of a stout oak on the west side. A circular driveway in front of the house led from the main street. This mansion was certainly fancier than Alistair's home in Clay County.

"Pa at the store?" Beans asked his brother.

"Where else?"

"Is Ma …?"

Beans didn't get to finish, because the white door swung open, and a woman in a collarless day dress of red and green calico, no hoop, raced out, lifting the hems of her skirts, and screaming: "Benedict! Benedict! God be praised! God be praised!" She wasn't tall at all. Beans had to kneel a little so she could kiss his cheek.

Two Negroes, one white-haired woman, the other a husky fellow with a shaved head, maybe the age of Alistair's pa, stopped in the doorway.

Dabbing her eyes, Mrs. Kimbrough backed away, almost said something, before she realized that her son hadn't come alone.

"Found these scamps on the road." Smiling, Beans again made the introductions. "They're bound north. I told them that you set the finest table in Saint Clair County."

"Goodness." She curtsied, and tried to wipe the flour off her cheeks and hands. "You are most welcome, though I dare say my son has exaggerated. Besides …"—her head tilted toward the two slaves—"Reginald and Dilly do most of the cooking."

Alistair managed to smile, yet couldn't think of any proper response, but Quantrill slid from the saddle and began speaking all sorts of things. First, he pointed out that unless he was mistaken, he detected flour on Mrs. Kimbrough's hands, so she must have plenty of say in some of the food. Be that as it may,

Quantrill continued, she need not go to any trouble, that it was too hot for a lady of the house to be cooking for strangers.

"It's no trouble at all," she said. "You gentlemen wash up … you especial, Benedict. You look a fright, son. Did they not feed you in that army? How long are you home? Goodness, we were so worried after hearing of that dreadful fight near Springfield! Darius, you must run and fetch your father from the mercantile."

"He won't come," the younger brother mumbled, but Mrs. Kimbrough didn't hear.

"Benedict, show your friends to the washroom." She hurried back inside.

"You can stable your horse behind the house," the brother said. He grinned at Beans. "You don't look like a soldier."

"Anybody been snooping around here?" Beans asked. "Anybody been asking about me?"

Darius straightened. "No." His eyes brightened with a look of devilment. "What have you done?"

"Nary a thing. Go tell Pa I'm home. And tell me how sick he looks when you give him the news."

* * * * *

Everything about Beans Kimbrough changed the moment he returned home. No longer did he speak like some bumpkin, losing the ain'ts, the dropped Gs. As Alistair and Quantrill sat in the parlor, sipping tea and exchanging pleasantries with Mrs. Kimbrough while chicken and biscuits baked in the summer kitchen, Beans disappeared to his upstairs bedroom. He returned in striped britches, silk shirt, gray waistcoat, puffy blue tie, and Wellington boots. Duds liked that shamed Alistair, in his rags and filthy bare feet.

Quantrill had been bragging on the house, on Mrs. Kimbrough's lovely dress, but now he stopped in midsentence, rising from the leather chair, and bowing at Beans Kimbrough.

"You clean up nicely." Quantrill winked. "A man could mistake you for a gentleman." Quickly he looked at Mrs. Kimbrough. "I jest, ma'am. Your son is well-mannered, well-read, well-schooled. We are proud of him, and his service, but I think we should thank you for all that he is."

Alistair's mouth dropped open. Criminy, Quantrill had just met both of them the other day, and he was speaking like they'd fought Lyon's Federals together, and then some.

With a snort, Beans moved across the rug, bowing again at his mother, and sliding into a chair across from Alistair, who happened to catch a glimpse at the pocket Colt revolver the waistcoat couldn't quite hide.

"So you taught school, Mister Hart?" Mrs. Kimbrough asked. Quantrill was using the Charley Hart name again.

"Yes, ma'am. As I was saying, I grew up in Kentucky, but wanderlust took hold of me, and I journeyed West. Thought I would make my pile in Utah, then in Colorado's gold country, but …"—his head shook—"my piles did not attain much height. So I returned to what I did best, and that is teach school. In Stanton Township. In Lykins County." He laughed again. "I dare say I have been unable to determine which was more rude, the schoolhouse itself, or the children of Abolitionists that I labored to educate. By and by, I taught in Lawrence, too."

"Lawrence?" Beans leaned forward in his chair.

"As I explained earlier, Benedict, I had my reasons for living amongst Abolitionists and villainy."

"I visited Lawrence a few times myself." Beans winked at his mother, whose face paled.

"We need not bring up those sordid excursions, Son." She was standing, determined to return to the kitchen, when the front door opened. Then everyone stood, except Beans, who had found a cigar and busied himself clipping the end.

"Horatio." Mrs. Kimbrough hurriedly greeted her husband with a bow, not a kiss, took his silk hat, and left to check on supper. The man dropped a cane in a can in the corner, loosened his tie, and strode across the room to a decanter. He did not speak until he had gulped down two fingers of whiskey.

"Is that the uniform of the Missouri State Guard?" Mr. Kimbrough asked.

"Got mustered out." Beans' rough language had returned. He struck a match on his boot, and the cigar flared as he began puffing.

"Well I can imagine." Horatio Kimbrough set the empty glass on the table, then looked at Alistair and Quantrill. "I did not see your name in the butcher's bill of dead in the *Herald*."

"To your bitter disappointment, I warrant."

Turning away from his son, the father glowered at Alistair and Quantrill. "Were you two mustered out as well?"

Beans inherited his height from his father—the man had ducked through the threshold—but not his eyes. Horatio Kimbrough's were darker than a crow, hard and menacing, and, unlike his two raw-boned sons, his arms and chest were stout. The top of his bald head glistened with sweat, but he didn't seem the type of man Alistair would call a coward. He certainly couldn't picture this man cowering behind a store's cash box six days a week.

"I got paroled," Alistair stammered. "After I was captured."

"And I, Mister Kimbrough, did not have the honor of fighting with General Price at Wilson's Creek," Quantrill said coolly. "Still, I am recruiting men to defend Missouri from Yankee tyrants and Kansas jayhawkers."

Turning, Mr. Kimbrough snorted and spit into the empty fireplace. "We have nothing to fear from Yankees or Kansans."

At this, Quantrill stiffened.

"What we should fear are the fire-breathers on both sides," Mr. Kimbrough was saying. "Secession was pure folly. Almost as outrageous as the notion of freeing slaves."

Quantrill's lips pressed tightly, but the mood relaxed as Beans blew smoke toward the ceiling and laughed.

"How was business at the store today, Pa?"

Now it was Horatio Kimbrough whose face reddened, but before anyone else could speak, the old Negress entered the parlor, signaling her approach by ringing a silver bell. When she stuck her head through the open door, she announced: "Supper time, gentleman. Miz Miranda say y'all come before it gets cold."

* * * * *

The food was wonderful, but they could have served burned acorns, and Alistair would have thought they tasted better than roast beef with extra gravy. The biscuits weren't as fluffy as his mother's, but he couldn't remember the last time he had eaten chicken that was not mixed with dumplings. Mrs. Kimbrough had brought out gold-rimmed china, and silver, too. Plus, they had a bowl full of fresh-picked peaches for dessert.

Felt like a prince, Alistair did, dining at a palace.

No one spoke during supper. Everyone kept quiet like at a prayer meeting. A body could hardly get a word in when the Durants gathered around a table full of victuals. Maybe Quantrill and Mr. Kimbrough were still fuming over their politics. Maybe Beans and his father despised one another, but respected Mrs. Kimbrough enough not to torment her. At least, not at the supper table. Even Darius, Beans' little brother, who had missed the parlor talk, just stuffed his mouth with food, and never tried needling his brother.

All of which suited Alistair to a T. He helped himself to three servings, then plucked two peaches from the bowl, and ate. A little hard, not quite ripe, but nothing tasted better than a peach.

"You are welcome to spend the night," Mr. Kimbrough said after Mrs. Kimbrough had left and the servants had removed all the plates, leaving only a pot of coffee and three china cups and saucers.

"Why, thank you, Daddy," Beans said with a smirk.

"I speak to your friends," Mr. Kimbrough said stiffly.

"But of course."

"If you'd like to make yourself useful, you and Darius can see to Mister Hart's horse. And our stock as well."

Beans laughed without humor, looked at his brother, and scraped the legs of his chair on the floor as he rose. "Reckon he's sendin' you with me, Darius," he said, "to make sure I don't steal no horse."

Beans shunned his vest and tie, making sure his father spotted the little revolver, drained his glass of tea, and followed Darius through the side door.

* * * * *

It had been a long time since Alistair had slept this late. Last time he took sick, Alistair remembered, had been back home, not counting the dysentery down Springfield way. And he couldn't ever remember sleeping past 8:00. That, he had to blame on the feathered bed.

He washed his face, rubbed his teeth with a wet handkerchief, dressed, and hurried downstairs to the smell of fresh coffee.

"Good morning, Master Durant," Mrs. Kimbrough said, then began sorting through a tray of silverware. "Dilly, pour him some coffee. Do you take cream? Sugar?" She wasn't listening, though, for an answer. She stared at the forks and knives and spoons. Shook her head. Started over again, counting out loud.

The old slave woman, Dilly, waited for Alistair. "Black's fine," he said.

"Gots scones, too," she said. "Boys ate all the ham, but I can fry more. Eggs, too."

"A scone's aplenty." His stomach remained full from supper.

"Mister Hart left already," Mrs. Kimbrough said. "Wanted to cover some ground before the day turned blessedly hot. Said to tell you good-bye and …" She shook her head. "Dilly … did you or Reginald …?" She let out a sigh of exasperation.

Dilly was back, placing a plate of scones—more than the one—and a cup of steaming coffee in front of Alistair.

"Goodness gracious," Mrs. Kimbrough said. She studied the tray of silver in disbelief.

Mr. Kimbrough entered the room, dropping two newspapers on the table, nodding slightly at Alistair.

"Yes, ma'am?" Dilly asked. She waited. "Miz Miranda?"

Mrs. Kimbrough blinked absently, not even noticing the slave.

"Miz Miranda?" Dilly said again.

Alistair stopped eating. Mr. Kimbrough looked away from the newspapers.

"What is it?" Mr. Kimbrough demanded.

That got his wife's attention. "Oh, it's ... nothing."

"It's that son of yours," Mr. Kimbrough snapped.

"No. No, Horatio. I've just misplaced some silverware."

"And a china cup, Miz Miranda!" the male servant, Reginald, called from the next room.

"That boy's a thief!" Mr. Kimbrough roared.

"Benedict would not steal from his own family." Beans' mother defended her son. "No ... No. I've simply misplaced them."

"Fiddlesticks," Mr. Kimbrough said.

"I know our son, Horatio."

"Then that Charley Hart." The man's fists tightened. "I did not care for his looks. Not one iota."

"He is a perfect gentleman."

Kimbrough yelled for coffee, then found Alistair biting into a scone. "Maybe this boy's the culprit."

"Sir?" Bits of blueberries and bread flew across the table. Alistair blushed, started to wipe up the mess, but Dilly was already seeing to it. She couldn't hide her grin.

Slurping coffee, washing down the food but spilling more down the front of his shirt, Alistair managed to say: "I haven't taken ... I didn't ... I ... wouldn't ..."

Reginald brought coffee to Mr. Durant as Beans' mother tried to fight battles on all fronts: "Horatio, please do not insult our guests. Just eat your breakfast, Master Durant. Dilly, would you look in the pie safe? I know it seems silly, but I just don't know where I could have put that silver."

"Or the coffee cup," Reginald added.

"Might have been Charley Hart," Mr. Kimbrough said. "Explains why he left before first light. But I think it was your son. He's probably already traded it for grog."

"I have simply misplaced everything," she said, adding, "addled as I am." That comment appeared to be directed at Mr. Kimbrough.

"And I certainly do not trust this barefoot brigand from Cass County."

Mr. Kimbrough's dark eyes felt like daggers, but Alistair couldn't help himself. "Clay County," he corrected.

Which caused one of the slaves to stifle a laugh by coughing.

Luckily Mr. Kimbrough hadn't heard. His eyes narrowed, and he pointed a spoon at Alistair. "You ate your peach," he said in a threatening tone, "skin and all."

"So did that Mister Hart, Horatio," his wife reminded.

All Alistair could do now was stare blankly at the merchant.

Beans Kimbrough's pa glanced at the front pages of both newspapers, sipped from his cup, shook his head, and finally trained those mean dark eyes on Alistair.

"Never trust a man, or boy, who eats the skin of a peach."

Seems just plain silly, Alistair thought. He'd never heard of such superstitions. A peach might be fuzzy, but there was nothing wrong eating it. He'd been doing that since he had teeth.

Time to skedaddle. Alistair wished he hadn't slept so late. Wanted to know why he'd ever lit out with Beans Kimbrough and William Quantrill.

"Well, I should be taking my leave," Alistair announced. "I have a long way to walk home."

"Young man, you finish your coffee," Mrs. Kimbrough said. "Dilly, pack Master Durant a sack. Cheese. Crackers. The rest of the scones. They'll just get moldy here. Some ham, too. And peaches. Skin and all!"

"You needn't ..."

"Hush up." She stared again at the tray of silver, pursing her lips, unable to comprehend what had happened to those missing utensils.

"I'll check that bag on his way out the door," Mr. Kimbrough said without looking up. "No telling what else of ours might find its way out of our front door." He didn't appear to be joking.

All Alistair could do was shake his head, and let out a mirthless chuckle. He expected a similar welcome home from his own father.

CHAPTER FOUR

If he lived twice as long as Methuselah, he'd never figure out Able Gideon Durant. Here Alistair came home, having lost his shotgun to the Yanks, after sneaking out in the middle of the night, high-tailing it all the way down to Jefferson City to enlist. Here he came, barefoot and blistered, sweaty and stinking to high heaven, and the first person he saw on the farm was his pa.

Here came his father, dropping the hoe in the garden, leaping over the split-rail fence, tossing off his battered straw hat, yelling at the dogtrot cabin for Ma and the sisters to hurry out and fetch a pitcher of well water. Pa, who Alistair considered the only Union man living in Clay County, put those thick arms on Alistair's shoulders, and pulled him close. Practically crushed the breath out of his lungs, then pushed him away an arm's length, saying: "Let me get a look at you ... but ... tarnation, I must got dirt in my eyes."

Ma and his sisters had nothing in their eyes. Nothing but tears. Portia and Roberta, the two youngest, stood back hugging each other, Portia saying, "I told you he wasn't killed," and Roberta, wiping her eyes, muttering something Alistair couldn't quite hear. Cally, by all rights an old maid two years Alistair's senior, wiped her hands on her apron, alternately nodding while shaking her head, letting the tears cut rivers through the dirt on her face. Then there was his mother, Persis, bawling like a newborn, wetting his cheeks with kisses, and practically cracking all the ribs his father hadn't squashed.

Over his mother's sobs, he could make out part of his kid sisters' conversation.

"I never thought he was dead."

"Did, too."

"No. Just that Tommy Cobb said he heard Frank James say he saw our brother dead on the battlefield."

"Tommy Cobb used to live in Chicago. You can't trust what no boy from Chicago says."

What does Tommy Cobb know? Alistair thought. Tommy hadn't joined the Missouri State Guard. Far as Alistair knew, Tommy was still clearing fields along Shoal Creek. Frank James had been there, but, like Alistair, was sicker than a dog when the battle commenced. Measles, he thought. Maybe mumps. Frank, who lived on a farm about five miles closer to Centerville, had seen as much action in battle as Alistair had. Last he'd seen of Frank, he was still sick, waiting his parole from the Yankees.

Pa told Roberta and Portia to hush up, and Ma kept muttering: "God be praised. God be praised. God be praised."

When she pulled away, Persis Durant touched her trembling lips, then put the back of her hand on Alistair's cheeks. "Lands sake," she said, "I believe you need a razor."

"Ma," Alistair said, "I'm seventeen years old."

Smiling, his father ran his hand on Alistair's other cheek. "You're two months passed sixteen, son, but I dare say Persis is right. You do need a shave."

"What he needs," Cally said, "is a bath. And them clothes burnt."

Which was just like Cally.

* * * * *

"I'm not a Republican, Son. Doubt if you'd find any Republican in Missouri this side of Saint Louis. Voted for Stephen Douglas, I did. Thought he could keep a lid on things. But now …" His head shook wearily. "The Little Giant himself is dead. Much like the Union itself, I fear."

Freshly washed—even behind his ears—and wearing clean duck trousers and a homespun shirt, Alistair stared in disbelief. He hadn't heard of Stephen Douglas' death. Hadn't heard anything much since joining the Confederate militia in June. They were sitting outside for supper. Too blasted hot to eat indoors, but the table had been set with Davenport ironstone, not tin, as well as store-bought sugar, things usually reserved for Christmas and Easter, or when Grandma Agnes visited from Gallatin.

"You understand," Able Durant went on, "that I oppose Secession. Always have. I remember joining up with a militia in Kentucky before we moved west, and I remember saluting the Kentucky flag and the Stars and Stripes. Hanged if I'll ever fire on that flag, Son."

"We're glad you didn't," his mother interjected.

"I didn't do much of anything," Alistair said.

"But you stood your ground." Able Durant's head nodded firmly. "Did what you thought right. That's what a father wants from his son. Persis, pass our son some more peas."

Right? Alistair didn't know if he thought the Confederacy was right. He had joined up because he figured war would be some adventure. Certainly the idea of battle and glory seemed a whole lot more appealing that hoeing fields, digging potatoes, and shucking corn. About the only thing that satisfied Alistair was working horses, which reminded him. After his mother had filled his empty plate with more peas, he leaned back in his chair, and stared at the corral.

"How's that black mare coming …?" He didn't finish. The front legs of the chair fell forward, and he almost shot to his feet. "Where's?"

"Jayhawkers," his father said.

"You mean redlegs," Cally said with contempt.

"Same thing," Able Durant muttered. "Come by when I was in Centerville one eve. Took the black, took all the horses."

His mother shook her head. "Rode off with three of your pa's best Poland Chinas."

Roberta added: "Even took a crock of honey."

"Said we was lucky," Portia said, "'cause they was leaving us the house and barn."

Alistair held the butter knife in his hands, gripping the handle so hard his knuckles whitened. He felt his entire body trembling. When at last he released the knife, letting it drop to the table, his eyes found his father. "But you're not a Secesh. And there are no slaves here to be stolen."

"Some of Doc Jennison's men," Cally said. "Called themselves 'volunteer citizen scouts' and ..."

"Kansas trash," his mother said, which was as close as Persis Durant ever came to profanity.

"They raided Independence first," Cally said. "Broke into a shop there, stole a bunch of red Moroccan sheepskin leather, which they made into leggings. Redlegs."

Alistair had trouble getting his point across. "But they had no right."

"Yankees give them the right," Cally said, and her eyes had hardened more than Alistair's. "Right to steal, plunder. It don't make no never mind to any bluecoat. They pillage and torment, and say it's all for the good of the Union."

"But ..."

"Kansas trash," his mother repeated.

"Took that crock of honey," Roberta said again. "Full it was, too. Didn't even get a chance to taste it on a biscuit."

He sank into his chair. "When did this happen?"

"Three nights back," his father said. "Oh, I reported it to the sheriff, sent word to Confederate and Union authorities, even posted a letter to this Senator James Henry Lane out of Lawrence, Kansas. He seems to be in charge of some Kansas Brigade. Lot of good any of it'll do."

Alistair tested the other name, the one Cally had mentioned. "Doc Jennison."

"I heard them mention Six Mile House," Cally said. "Some place in Kansas. Appears to be the place they operate out of."

"A den of thieves," his mother said.

He tried to carve that into his brain. Doc Jennison. Redlegs. Six Mile House. Lawrence. James Henry Lane. Kansas Brigade.

"War's come to Missouri, Son," Able Durant said softly. "But it won't be like that battle down Springfield way. Won't be nothing of the kind. It'll be just like the border wars with John Brown and John Reid. Border ruffians and …"

"Kansas trash," his mother cut in.

"It'll be worser than that," Cally said. "Mark my words, it'll be worser than those border wars ever was."

He stared at the peas. Which was all he could do. His appetite had vanished.

"Don't go off your feed," his father said after a lengthy silence. "You've lost enough weight. And all we're out is some good horses, a blind mule, a few pigs, and honey. That can all be replaced. No, this is a joyful time. Reason to celebrate."

"Can we go to the barn raising?" Roberta asked. "Tomorrow night?"

"That's a crackerjack idea," Able Gideon said. "Be good for us all."

* * * * *

A few Mormons still lived in Clay County, and, if you looked hard enough, you could fine some Presbyterians and Methodists, but Baptists were thicker than June bugs on a windowsill in summer. Most of them, however, weren't hard-shell. In fact, Alistair would call them backsliders. As long as it wasn't Sunday, most didn't object to a quart of London porter or jug of corn liquor. Nor did they mind dancing.

Best way, they'd say, to break in a new barn.

His first dance had been at a barn raising the day after he'd returned home, and now, in early October, he found himself at another. This time, however, they were building a new barn for Jared McBride. Redlegs had burned down his barn three nights earlier.

Since coming home, Alistair had caught only smatterings of war news. Pap Price had won a couple more victories, at Big Dry Wood Creek and at Lexington, but whisperings suggested that the Rebels couldn't hold the state. Certainly there were enough Federal troops all around western Missouri to make that sound more gospel than gossip. Most reports centered on raids: Kansas redlegs burning out farms; Missouri partisans ambushing small patrols here and there.

Just a minute earlier, he had heard Hobart Kennedy ask his father: "Have you heard about Osceola?"

That had grabbed Alistair's attention, but before he heard anything else, Lucy Cobb had lured him away.

Alistair had finished doing the "Amelia's Waltz," and was leading Lucy to the punch bowls as most of the folks got ready for the "Reel of Springfield." His father and Mr. Hobart had disappeared in the crowd, but he happened to see Lucy's brother, Tommy, filling a tin cup. He'd wanted to needle Tommy since lighting home.

"Hey, Tommy," Alistair said, finding a handkerchief to mop his sweaty face.

Tommy turned. His stringy corn-silk hair had been freshly shorn, and he sported the beginnings of a mustache. He also carried a pistol in his waistband. Missouri sure had changed. Tommy looked all grown up, and he wasn't the only one heeled at this barn dance.

"Hey, Alistair." Tommy offered a good-natured grin.

"I look pretty good for a dead man, don't I?"

"What you talkin' about?"

He didn't get to answer because four bluecoats walked into the barn. The fiddling stopped. Mr. Jared McBride—it was his barn that had just been put up—stepped out from the throng of dancers and said: "No Yankees were invited to this dance, Capt'n, especially from your ... ahem ... brigade, sir."

The captain, a short, squat man with a flowing mustache and beard, bowed mockingly. "I need no invitation, sir, when I seek bushwhacking vermin for ambushing a Union patrol at a farm near Independence."

"If it's vermin you seek, you'll find 'em at Six Mile House in Wyandotte County, Capt'n," someone said.

"Or Lawrence," another voice added.

The Yankee captain smoothed his mustache. He announced in a warning voice: "There is a cowardly ruffian in these parts who appears to be in command. We believe he is called Quantrill. 'Tis him that we seek. No one else, ladies and gentleman."

At the mention of Quantrill's name, Alistair spilled punch all over his clean shirt, absent-mindedly handed the half-full cup to Lucy, and took a step closer to the Yankees, just to make sure he'd heard correctly.

"Are you Quantrill?" the Yankee asked.

It took a while before the question registered. "No."

The other bluecoats chuckled. "I didn't expect," the captain said, "this yellow bushwhacker to be so noble. Who are you then?"

"Me?" He felt awkward, realizing that every eye in the barn had lighted on him. "Me? Nobody. I mean, I'm Alistair Durant."

"A hayseed's name if ever I heard one," a pockmarked private said, and spit tobacco juice onto a platter of fried chicken.

The captain kept walking, not stopping till he was almost standing on the toes of Alistair's boots. He smelled of whiskey. His eyes were bloodshot, and when he opened his mouth, Alistair saw a mix of gold fillings, empty spaces, and rotting teeth.

"But you know of this Quantrill, don't you?"

Before Alistair could deny anything, the Yankee went on: "Come now, boy. Your eyes have betrayed you. This villain rides with some of Morgan Walker's boys, and other Secesh vermin. Come now, you know of Quantrill. You probably ride with him and all that Rebel trash."

"I got paroled," Alistair said weakly. "After Wilson's Creek. I don't ride with anybody."

"He can't," a familiar voice added. "Since y'all done stole all our horses!"

Cally stepped beside him. That's when Alistair looked down, and saw the man's kersey pants stuck into leggings made of Moroccan sheepskin leather.

"Well," the captain said, "a bushwhacking hussy with a big mouth. The boys and me know how to teach trollops a lesson or two."

He started to reach for her, but never made it.

Something snapped inside him. Alistair grabbed the bluecoat's arm, jerked him forward and down while bringing up his own knee. He meant to smash his face, but only caught the blow-hard's chin. In the corner of his eye, he saw Tommy Cobb—no, it was Lucy—throwing the tin cup at the other redlegs. Tommy had filled his hand with something else, a little Sharps pistol, which flooded the barn with smoke and, for such a small weapon, a deafening explosion.

That stopped the other Yankees from moving. Alistair focused on the captain, who was crawling away while reaching for the revolver on his hip. The clasp of his holster was fastened. Alistair moved deliberately, lifted his leg, and brought the heel of his boot down hard on the redleg's left hand. He heard the bones crunch, heard the Yankee scream, then Alistair kicked him in the face. Blood spurted. Someone laughed. Another shrieked in terror.

The last time Alistair had tangled with anyone had been with Mr. Richard McCoy's son, Dill, seven, eight years ago. They hadn't even thrown a punch, just wrestled till Mr. McCoy separated them and made them shake hands. He couldn't recall what had led to that brawl, and, afterward, he had cried on his mother's shoulder, feeling sick about it all. This was different. Alistair felt nothing.

The captain fell on his back, his eyes rolling into the back of his head, and Alistair reached down, unfastened the holster, drew the Remington revolver. Only it wasn't Alistair moving. It had to be someone else. He felt as if he were watching himself in a dream. He heard the Remington's hammer come to full cock. Saw the barrel pointed at the Yank's bloody face.

Then he heard Cally saying: "He ain't worth it, Brother. You kill him, you'll just make things harder on the McBrides, and they seen hardships enough as it is."

No dream. He felt sick to his gut. Thought he might throw up all over that miserable redleg. The barrel lowered, and he glanced at Cally, then at Lucy, finally at the other ashen-faced Yanks now cornered by at least a dozen Clay County farmers.

He caught bits of conversation. Mr. McBride telling one of the Yankees that if Quantrill were such a coward, how come he had gone to the Independence constable after some fracas near town, telling the squire that Quantrill admitted he was in charge, and that the two men the Yanks had jailed had nothing to do with the little set-to with jayhawkers. Richard McCoy saying that Quantrill and his men had saved farmers from redlegs. Someone offered three cheers for Captain Quantrill. Another sang out huzzahs for Alistair Durant and Tommy Cobb.

Tommy Cobb stood at his side, taking the Remington from his hand, easing down the barrel, then handing back the heavy revolver. "Welcome home," he said.

Alistair's head shook. He heard his sister saying: "Things ain't like they used to was."

CHAPTER FIVE

A tick couldn't have slipped into their hideout.

Say anything you wanted to about Clay County, or much of western Missouri, but in those parts, a thicket was a thicket. Dense, coarse, hilly, practically impregnable. The sun's rays barely made it into the small clearing where Alistair Durant and Tommy Cobb had been forced to hide. A body had to know how to dodge the briars and brambles, or where to crawl under them, and which deer trail wouldn't dead-end, to reach the little clearing, and then have enough sense to find the way back out.

The weather had turned cool, and it had rained so hard last night, water still dripped off the branches and reddening leaves. Hearing the sound of boots splashing in water, Tommy Cobb drew and cocked the Remington taken off that redleg at the McBrides' place, while Alistair unsheathed a Bowie knife. Both crouched in the shadows.

"Tommy!" a voice called out. "Alistair. It's us."

Letting out a hoarse breath, Alistair slid the big knife back into his boot, and came out of his hiding place. A minute later, Lucy Cobb crawled under a rotting elm, pushing a basket of food in front of her. Next came Cally. Tommy went straight for the basket, grinning, while Alistair helped his sister and Lucy to their feet. A third figure suddenly appeared, and Alistair reached for the knife as Tommy dropped the basket and leveled the .44.

"It's all right," Cally said. "He's with us. Says he knows you, and I reckon he does. We questioned him enough."

The face of a man looked up. Beard stubble darkened his face, but those green eyes remained brilliant.

"'Mornin', Alvin," Beans Kimbrough said.

* * * * *

Like wolves, they tore into corn pone with molasses, cold salt pork, washing down the grub with bitter and cold coffee. Wiping their hands on their filthy pants legs. The hideout reeked, and when Alistair looked at the two girls and Beans, he felt shamed. They lived like animals. Acted like animals.

"You ain't told me how come you're here," he said to Beans. *Ain't.* Alistair shook his head. He was at it again. His mother had insisted that one of her children get proper schooling, when the farm and horses could spare it, so the wife of the Baptist minister over at New Hope had made sure Alistair learned to read and write, do his ciphers, and speak properly, not like some Missouri ruffian. That lady had even gotten Alistair interested in Shakespeare. He could speak like a gentleman, too, even though it had caused him considerable pain at church, at gatherings, and at the regular subscription school. Come to think of it, that's what had started his row with Dill McCoy all those years back.

"Talk fancy for us, Alistair," Dill had said, and when the other kids had laughed, Alistair had lit into him.

Beans Kimbrough's face hardened. "You didn't hear?"

Tommy Cobb dunked a hunk of pone into his coffee. "Hear what?" he managed to say before filling his mouth.

"About Osceola?"

Alistair glanced at his sister, who bowed her head.

"They burned it down."

"Burned what?" Tommy asked. "Who ...?"

"Burned Osceola. Nothing left but ashes. Jim Lane's Kansas *banditti*."

"Redlegs?" Alistair asked.

"Redlegs? I don't know nothin' about no redlegs. No, jayhawkers. Kansas rapscallions. They called 'emselves a Union army, but they were thieves. Arsonists. Murderers." Tears welled in his eyes. An eternity passed before he regained enough composure to continue.

"We'd heard Lane was raidin' towns. I told Pa we should maybe prepare ... hide our money and stuff ... but he said he had nothing to fear. Just like him. So on the twenty-third last, we hear shots. Didn't have much of an army to defend us, so the Rebs retreated, and in rode Lane and his men. Frightenin' lookin' cuss, Lane is. I was runnin' to see what was causin' all the ruction, and, I mean to tell you, what I see gives me a fright. And I don't frighten easily, mind you. Torches. Just comin' down off cemetery ridge. Must've been hundreds of 'em. And those boys are howlin' like Injuns. I knowed then we was in trouble. Big trouble. I starts to run, but gets captured by a couple of Kansans. I'm thinkin' they'll just shoot me dead ... but Lane orders 'em to help with the cannon. And they start shellin' the courthouse. Then buildings. After they've stole what they can get out of 'em.

"We figured all they'd do was steal. Maybe rob the bank. Free some of our darkies. And, sure, they done that. But then they gathered a dozen men. Lane yells out ... 'We must burn out leprosy or cholera or any disease, and treason is such a disease.' He says these men are bein' tried for treason. He lines 'em up on the square, and shoots 'em down like dogs. Lane just didn't bark that order. He fired his revolver till it was empty. Killed nine. Must've thought the other three was dead, too. And just left 'em there, settin' all the businesses on the square afire."

Another long silence.

Then: "You remember Reginald and Dilly? Our two slaves? Last I saw of them, they were in the back of a wagon loaded down with our piano, curtains, and things they'd gathered from one of the churches." His short laugh held no humor. "Looked as scared as my mother.

"You see, by then Lane's men had found whiskey. Bunch of the barrels got staved in, others dumped into the river. Lot of the liquor spilled onto the streets, and you should've seen those Kansans. Lappin' up that liquor in the street like cur dogs. Fillin' their canteens. Others found jugs and bottles in the saloons. Started drinkin' till half of 'em or better was drunker than skunks. They went from home to home, robbin', and ... and ... and ..." He shuddered, wet his lips, and looked at Alistair. "I could use some liquor."

"I'm sorry," Alistair said. "We don't have anything stronger than day-old, cold coffee."

"They burn your home?" Tommy asked.

"They burned everything. By the time they left that night, there wasn't hardly nothin' left." Beans shook his head, staring at his muddy boots. "I hear Jim Lane yell that Osceola is a den of Secessionists and slaveholders and must be purged. But ..." Again his head shook. "But that ain't true. You met Pa. You saw what he was like. He was a Union man. Slaveholder, sure, but there ain't nothin' wrong with that. Yet he wouldn't never leave the Union."

"My pa's the same way," Alistair said.

"They killed him," Beans said hollowly.

"What?" Alistair dropped his coffee cup. "But ..."

"They didn't care. Oh, he wasn't shot for treason. They killed him when he blocked the door of the mercantile. Said he tried to shoot 'em, but Pa hadn't fired a gun in a 'coon's age. Dragged him back into the buildin', and when they was done pillagin', they burned it to the ground, too. With Pa inside."

Alistair heard a sniff, turned to find Lucy dabbing her eyes with the hems of her skirt, saw Cally's head bowed, her hands clasped as in prayer. He looked over at Tommy Cobb, but could not read his face.

"I'm sorry, Beans," Alistair said.

"Never … figured Pa would … die … on me." Beans' voice cracked. He shuddered, wiped his face, and looked around. "Some place you got here, Alistair." For once, Beans hadn't butchered Alistair's name.

"What brings you to Clay County?" Alistair asked, trying to change the subject, though he thought he knew.

"Got word from my Uncle Morgan Walker that some boys 'round here have been makin' things miserable for the Yankees. I aim to see Jim Lane dead. Might be you've heard of these partisans."

"Quantrill," Alistair said softly.

"His name has been bandied around some."

For the first time, Alistair noticed Beans Kimbrough's dress. Boots with spurs. Blue trousers, a calico shirt, vest, and hat. Yet around his waist two revolvers were belted, with another stuck in the waistband. The trousers were wool, blue, part of a Federal uniform. So was the darker vest, which had two holes to the right of the center brass buttons.

"I'd say you've found Quantrill already," Alistair said.

Beans smiled. "You're a bright boy. He didn't start out as leader of our army, but, yeah, he's worked his way up to captain. We heard what had happened to y'all. Ol' Charley Hart sent me here, see if you had a mind to join up with us. We'll make 'em Yankees pay. Kansans in particular."

Almost immediately, Tommy Cobb said: "I'm game."

Alistair glanced at his sister, at Lucy Cobb, then at the filth he called home. Yankees had posted a reward for him. Criminy, he was already outlawed. That parole he'd been given meant nothing. Yet still he looked at Cally.

"If I go," he said, "like as not it'll make things hot on y'all."

"Make it hot on them," she said.

CHAPTER SIX

Make it hot on them. All these months later, Cally's words still rang in Alistair's thoughts.

Down the winding road just south of Sni-A-Bar Township he walked. Three men on horseback behind him, not speaking, keeping their revolvers aimed at his back. March remained downright cold, and he wanted to stick his hands underneath the greatcoat, maybe inside his woolen trousers pockets, but the rawhide strips binding his wrists prevented that.

Make it hot? Alistair reckoned he had done that. Well, maybe he hadn't contributed much to the cause, but Quantrill and "the boys"—as they were being called by Southern supporters in Missouri—sure had.

* * * * *

Just a couple days after joining up with Quantrill, Alistair had gotten to see the elephant, as the saying went, when the Rebels ambushed a Yankee patrol at Manassas Gap. He had fired a few shots, though he didn't hit anyone, and most of the Yankees surrendered real quickly once the shooting had commenced. Quantrill's soldiers, called irregulars by Rebel military, and a lot worse by Kansans and

Federals, had relieved those bluecoats of their hardware and ammunition. Since winter was coming on, they'd taken their greatcoats, too. Alistair still wore the one he'd liberated. They'd also picked out the best horses, and a few boys had taken watches and coins. When it was all over, Quantrill had lined up the Yankees—maybe a dozen or more—and said: "I'm paroling you swine. Go back to your homes. You're done with this war. But if I meet you in battle again, you shall never see another sunrise."

Later, the boys wouldn't be so charitable. Nor would jayhawkers and redlegs, if they had ever known mercy.

In fact, the first man Alistair had seen killed by the partisans hadn't been a bluecoat at all, but a Confederate deserter. Alistair had already forgotten the name of that rapscallion who had been stealing mules from Union families around Independence, which was well and good. The deserter had stolen some pretty fine horses, too, along with deeds, banknotes, even a couple of mortgages. Yet he wasn't too bright a criminal, and when he had taken a pot shot at Quantrill along the Little Blue, his thieving days ended.

Bill Anderson had thrown a rope over a tree limp, letting Oll Shepherd tighten a noose around the fellow's neck. The man started a speech, but the boys soon grew bored, as it was cold by then, so Arch Clements had lashed the mule's rear with a quirt, ending that speech in midsentence.

"Boys," Quantrill had said as the wind blew the corpse this way and that, "it is time that we disband. Winter is coming along, and you have not seen your families in months. Go to them, but sleep with one eye open and a revolver under your pillow. Yankees will give us no rest. Be resourceful, be diligent, be smart. We will gather in the spring. Alistair. Corn Cobb."

By that time, everyone had started calling Tommy "Corn Cobb".

"Yes, Captain."

Quantrill had handed a carpetbag to Alistair. "You will see these items find their way into the rightful owners."

"Capt'n, 'em notes and truck was taken offen Yankee lovers." George Todd never ceased complaining. Alistair had never cared much for that rowdy ex-mason.

"We do not wage war on civilians, Mister Todd," Quantrill had snapped.

* * * *

By the time Alistair had secured the grip behind his cantle, most of the men had ridden off. The boys knew better than stick around in one place for too long. They'd hit a patrol, then vanish in the thickets and hills, gathering later at some place the Yankees didn't know.

Beans Kimbrough had eased his roan mare closer to Tommy and Alistair.

"You goin' home?" Tommy had asked Beans.

"What home?" Beans had bitterly replied.

The rope slipped, and the corpse dropped a couple of inches.

"You really aim on takin' 'em things back to their owners?" Beans had asked.

"If I can find them," Alistair had said.

"What for?"

"It's what Capt'n Quantrill said," Tommy had shot back.

Beans had sprayed tobacco juice onto the hanged man's pants. "Yeah. After he went through 'em himself. Warrant he picked the cream of the crop for his own wallet."

"You're a big, lyin' dog!" Tommy had snapped, but, before Beans could get his dander up, Alistair had intervened.

"You might as well spend winter with us, Beans," he'd said. "I allow Cally would like to see you again."

At that Beans had grinned, although Alistair had no idea if his sister had even considered Beans Kimbrough.

Cally had, of course, stitched the wool shirt Alistair now wore under his greatcoat. Coarse wool, it was, not fancy, dark brown with tan trim, and plenty of pockets to hold extra cylinders for the revolvers he usually carried. Beans had one of those shirts, too, only Cally had taken time to embroider red roses and pink hearts on his pockets. So, it turned out, his sister had considered Beans Kimbrough, after all.

* * * * *

"Hold up there!"

The sharp command ended Alistair's memories, abruptly returning him to Sni-A-Bar and the three horsemen behind him. He stopped, hearing the clopping of hoofs on the far side of the hill to the north. They waited in a depression, the road shadowed by leafless trees that seemed thicker than stone walls. The wind moaned through those rattling limbs, and Alistair shivered when riders topped the hill. The Yankee leader raised his right arm, and the men behind him stopped. Another bluebelly said something, and the men kicked their mounts and eased down the slope, stopping a few feet in front of Alistair.

"What you got there?" a gray-bearded sergeant asked.

"Bushwhacker," came the reply behind Alistair. "Caught him down near Lone Jack. Figured to leave him at the jail at Blue Springs."

Another man, wearing a Hardee hat with a yellow ostrich plume stuck in the pinned-up side, spit, and fingered out the dip of snuff, wiping his hands on his greatcoat. Alistair glanced at him, then dropped his head, lifting his hands to pull his slouch hat down low. He felt himself shaking.

"Didn't you hear about General Halleck's orders?"

"Must've slipped by us, Capt'n."

Peering beneath the brim of his hat, Alistair saw the red leggings. He counted. *Six ... Seven ... Eight ... Nine ... Ten. Ten men.*

The captain was speaking, and Alistair felt his temper rising with each syllable. The redleg's nose was crooked, and he'd grown a ragged beard, but appeared to have recovered from the whipping Alistair had given him at the McBrides' farm back in October.

"Bushwhackers ain't soldiers," the captain was saying, "and ain't to be treated like soldiers. With honor." He snorted, wiped his nose. "You're supposed to hang them for what they is. Murderers and thieves. Not to mention cowards committing treason."

"Hell's fire, that suits us right down to the ground, Capt'n," a man behind Alistair said. "You got a rope? I see a tree with a solid branch right over yonder."

"You mind sayin' what outfit you're with?" It was the sergeant. Suspicious cuss, unlike the captain.

"Seventh Kansas Cavalry," one rider answered.

"Jennison's bunch?" the sergeant asked.

The man laughed. "Not hardly. We ride for Senator Lane. A real fightin' man."

"Oh." Alistair had to glance up, and despite the situation, found himself grinning at the sergeant, who bit his lip to keep from saying something. The Yank's ears were turning red, and the other riders looked angry, too. These men were redlegs. Probably friends of Doc Jennison.

Realizing that the captain was studying him, Alistair quickly dropped his head and focused on his boots.

"Wait a minute." It was the redleg captain's voice. Alistair heard the creaking of leather, the blowing of a horse, then footfalls. He felt chilled, not from the cold, but from the presence of this redleg scoundrel, who roughly jerked up Alistair's head, knocking off his hat.

Recognition was instant. "You!" the louse said.

He appeared to be missing a few more teeth. That pleased Alistair greatly.

"You filthy little …"

Alistair drove his fists into the redleg's stomach, heard the air whoosh out of the Kansan's lungs, and, as the captain doubled over, again Alistair brought up his knee, feeling the jaw break. By then Alistair was pulling free of the loosely wrapped rawhide, reaching inside the greatcoat, gripping one of his Navy Colts.

The three riders behind him had already reacted. Cole Younger got off the first shot. Frank James the second. Beans Kimbrough's voice rose above the din. "Let's start the ball, you bluecoat bastards!"

Alistair's ears rang as the Colt bucked in his hand. Horses screamed, bucked, bolted. Revolvers cracked behind Alistair, and balls whistled over his head. He could already smell gunpowder, and blood. More guns crackled in a deafening cannonade, for, by now, George Todd's patrol had appeared on the southern hill.

Four of the redlegs turned tail, galloping up the northern hill. Alistair wasted a shot after one of them, before realizing a more pressing concern. A bullet tugged at his greatcoat. He ducked, aimed, but the freckled face belonging to a kid probably younger than Alistair exploded in crimson. Someone else had killed that redleg. Alistair turned away from the dead kid, realized his Colt was already empty, and he shifted it to his left hand, pulling another revolver with his right.

At that moment, the top of the northern hill filled with other riders.

"Give them hell!" Quantrill yelled, and the dozen partisans disappeared in grayish white smoke.

Ten seconds later, it was all over. The ringing left his ears. Even the wind had stopped. A gunshot popped.

No, it wasn't over. Dill McCoy and Chris Kennard were walking by redlegs, sending balls in the heads of the dying and the already dead. Cole Younger put two Yankee horses out of their misery.

At his feet, the redleg captain moaned. Alistair looked at him, holstering his two Colts, and reached down, jerking the captain to his feet.

"Strip the dead of the uniforms!" Quantrill yelled out. "We can use them. Any wounded amongst my loyal troops?"

"Nary a scratch, Capt'n!"

"Excellent. Most ex—" He stopped, nudged Black Bess forward, and swung out of the saddle, handing the reins to Frank James. Excitedly he rushed to Alistair and the redleg captain.

"Alistair?" Quantrill said.

"The boy done well," Cole Younger said.

"Better than well," Frank James added. "He did great." Frank lifted his voice: "'But be not afraid of greatness. Some men are born great, some achieve greatness, and some have greatness thrust upon 'em.'"

That was just like Frank James. Always quoting Shakespeare, if not Scripture.

"What have we here?" Quantrill asked, his brow knotting as he glared at the battered face of the redleg captain.

The prisoner tried to talk, but the broken jaw refused to cooperate. All he could do was blubber.

"I am Captain Quantrill," Quantrill told the Kansan.

"He might …"—Alistair licked his lips—"tell us something about the Yanks, Captain."

"He can't tell us nothin'," Beans Kimbrough said. "Alistair practically knocked his jaw off."

"P-p-please," the redleg croaked.

"Hey." It was Tommy Cobb. He stepped over a corpse, and stood to Alistair's right, studying the mangled face of the officer. "This is the capt'n from the McBride farm. The son-of-a-bitch!" Tommy pulled his Navy, thumbed back the hammer, shoved the barrel into the redleg's gut.

"No! Please …" Broken jaw or not, everyone heard that. The captain tried to back away, but Cole Younger grabbed one arm, and Beans Kimbrough the other.

The redleg wet his britches.

"Let's see how good he talks with lead in his gut," Tommy Cobb said.

"No." Quantrill spoke firmly. "Holster your revolver, Mister Cobb."

"But …"

When Quantrill's eyes flamed, Tommy immediately lowered the hammer, and slid the Navy into a holster.

"We are not to be treated like prisoners of war," Frank James said.

The redleg sobbed.

"Tit for tat," Quantrill said, and turned to Alistair.

Alistair felt hot, numb, saw every eye on him. Even the dead Yankees seemed to stare at him.

"Muster him out, Mister Durant." Quantrill spoke evenly, smoothly.

"Sir?" Alistair's hands felt clammy.

Those usually calm eyes of William Quantrill hardened. "You remember this piece of Kansas filth, don't you, Durant?" Alistair couldn't look away from Quantrill. He heard the redleg stutter, beg, start to pray, yet Alistair could not turn from Quantrill.

"This is the man who made you an outlaw. And for what? Defending your sister, Mister Cobb's sister, the one you are sweet on. Do you not remember that night? Have you forgotten this man's outrage? His poltroonish behavior? He would have left the barn you had just raised at the McBrides in ashes. Would have rendered them homeless. He would have ravaged your sister. *And Lucy Cobb as well!* He is vermin. And he would have lynched you here, without trial, without anything. A man like this has no honor. Look at him!"

Alistair made himself stare into the terrified face.

"You've seen this fiend's handiwork all across our noble state. Abandoned farms. Smoldering ruins. Trampled crops. He has butchered our men. He has plundered homes of citizens true to the South. Kill him."

Tears flowed down the redleg's face, blood dripping from his mouth into the filthy beard.

"Kill him now!"

Suddenly the face changed, draining of what little color remained, and the prisoner sucked in a short breath. His eyes registered shock, yet almost instantly began to fog over with coming death.

"Now ... twist." Quantrill raised his fisted right hand, turning the wrist sharply.

Alistair looked down. He didn't remember unsheathing the Bowie knife, now stuck to the hilt into the redleg's belly.

"Twist!" Quantrill roared.

Alistair obeyed.

More blood spilled down the captain's busted jaw. Cole Younger and Beans Kimbrough jerked back the redleg, who fell onto his back, the eyes rapidly losing their life until they no longer saw the gray clouds.

"Good lad." Quantrill spoke in a fatherly whisper. "Good lad." Even softer. Quantrill put his arm around Alistair's shoulder. "That's a good soldier." He squeezed, but quickly broke away. "We must ride." His voice now boomed. "Mister Anderson reports a larger Yankee patrol on the road from Independence. Let us not tarry. Divide into threes, and meet at Crows Creek three days hence."

Alistair wiped the blade on the dead man's pants. That would have to do, he figured. For now. He'd give the blade a proper cleaning back in camp. As far as cleansing his soul, however …

"How was it?" Beans Kimbrough asked.

Alistair looked into Beans' green eyes. He felt cold, hollow, but said: "It was damned easy."

Beans laughed. "Next one," he said, "will be even easier."

CHAPTER SEVEN

Seemed like they'd been running forever.

Shortly after regrouping in Cass County, Quantrill had read Halleck's edict, with little emotion, just stating the facts as the Yank general saw things. Bushwhackers weren't soldiers at all, but criminals. Federal troops had the authority to dispatch them immediately. Summary justice. No trial necessary. Hang them or shoot them, just make sure they're dead.

Calmly Quantrill had folded the letter, and announced: "I accept this challenge. But every man must make his own choice. Stay with me and fight, or go home to your families and farms. I hold nothing against anyone who desires to leave."

Next, he had unsheathed a saber and drawn a line—"Just like Travis done at the Alamo!" young Dill McCoy had exclaimed.— and Alistair had followed the others across that line. Fifteen had left, but most of them would return soon. Yankees and Yankee lovers were making things mighty hard on anyone who'd once ridden with the partisan Rebs.

Sometimes, though, Alistair wished that he had left. And not returned.

Rain fell in hard, icy sheets, and the boys were already soaked, freezing as they clawed their way to the Jordan Lowe farmhouse. Most of their horses were gone, captured or killed by bluecoats, and they seemed to have been walking since Little Sni Creek. Maybe longer.

Quantrill burst through the door of the long-abandoned farm, and the door fell off its leather hinges, crashing onto the sod floor. George Todd picked up the rotting wood, propping it up against an open window. Other miserable, worn-out partisans filed into what would have to pass for shelter, Alistair among them, hearing rats scurry through holes in the rough planking. He couldn't see them. Couldn't see his hand in front of his face.

A lucifer flared, but only briefly.

"Douse that fire, man!" Quantrill snapped.

"Christ, Capt'n!" It sounded like Arch Clements.

"Haven't we had enough Yankee surprises?" Quantrill roared.

Alistair found a spot in the corner near the open doorway as more of the boys made their way inside. He lucked out. Water dripped on either side of him, but not on him.

"Damned roof here holds water worser than a sieve," Henry Wilson complained.

"That you, Alistair?" Beans Kimbrough asked.

"Yeah."

"Hell's fire, I thought you was dead."

"Almost." His left hand pressed against his side, which still leaked blood, though not as much as it had earlier.

Alistair slid down the wall, which creaked against his weight, pulled his legs close to his body, and rocked slowly, trying to keep warm.

* * * * *

Alistair almost cried out in pain.

"That better?" Beans asked as he tightened the knot on the strip of cloth.

"Wouldn't ... call ... it ... better." Alistair winced.

"Don't let this bandage stay on too long," Beans said. "That starts to mortify, and you'll be wishin' that ball had kilt you outright."

Lightning ripped across the sky, allowing Alistair a glimpse of Beans' face. He looked older, but, criminy, they'd all aged.

"Feels like we have been runnin' since January," Beans said.

"Only March," Tommy Cobb said.

"Huh?"

"Started in March." Although his side blistered with pain, Alistair could take regular breaths. He even managed to push the wet bangs out of his face without too much agony. "When we burned the bridge on the Little Blue."

"That was only last month?" Beans asked.

"Right after the capt'n killed that Dutchy sergeant," Tommy said from the other side of the open doorway.

Alistair shut his eyes, but couldn't rid his mind of the image from that day—the Yankee sergeant swinging off his horse, raising his hands in surrender. Quantrill loping Black Bess over, aiming his revolver, blowing out the Dutchman's brains, then wheeling around his horse, yelling: "Halleck has thrown down the gauntlet, boys, but we draw the first blood!"

It hadn't ended there. He could picture McCoy and Kennard dragging the keeper out of the tollhouse and straight to Quantrill. Not just the old man, either, but his son, or maybe grandson, a kid not seven or eight years old.

He could hear Clell Miller saying: "He's a Yankee spy!" Miller was even younger than Alistair, twelve at the most, though tall for his age and already smoking a corncob pipe and one fine shot with a revolver.

He could hear the tollkeeper crying out, "I'm a good Southern man!" and Quantrill's immediate response: "The jury has reached its verdict."

He could hear the report of Quantrill's pistol shot, could see the keeper falling dead with a bullet in his forehead, could hear the sobbing kid, see the boy kneeling by the side of the dead man. At least, he could also remember Quantrill preventing Clell Miller from putting a ball in the back of that kid's head.

Tommy Cobb snorted, spit, and stretched his boots across the damp floor. Rain water kept plopping on his hat.

"March twenty-second," Tommy said. "Then we rode to the Tate place, and that's where the fun began."

Alistair remembered that, too. The Second Kansas surrounding the place. Bullets riddling the house. Last he remembered seeing there was the Tate farm in flames as they fled into the timbers, gunning at Yankees, firing at shadows, probably shooting at themselves. Having split up, they had vamoosed to some other farm. This time, a Missouri cavalry unit had surprised them, sending them running again.

And again.

And again.

Forever. March 22 to April 15. Felt like forever.

"I don't allow as I'll ever get my fingers cleaned," Beans Kimbrough was saying. "Climbin' through all that mud to reach the top of that bluff on the Little Sni."

"Shut the hell up," Frank James snapped. "And get some sleep."

* * * * *

Sleep had come in fits, but finally Alistair found himself far from some abandoned Jackson County farm, a million miles from a thunderstorm. He was in the hayloft with Lucy Cobb.

"You brave boy," Lucy was saying, feeling his bandaged side, which no longer throbbed. Something else throbbed, and Lucy was leaning over, letting her curls fall into Alistair's face, and her lips were on his. Next thing he knew—criminy, her tongue was in his mouth—and Alistair's hands were slipping inside her dress, touching her unmentionables, trying to get those buttons to cooperate with his fingers. Only now somebody was knocking on the door, and he could hear Mr. Cobb's booming voice: "Lucy! Lucy! Hang your hide,

Alistair Durant, I got my shotgun!" Even though Alistair and Lucy knew they were about to get killed, they didn't stop. Not until ...

He jerked awake, hearing screams, curses. A gun roared beside him, ringing in his ears. Bullets thudded against the walls of the Jordan Lowe place. Or went through the rotting wood.

"I'm hit!" someone cried.

"Well," Cole Younger said, "what did you expect? This ol' house couldn't keep rain out. Think it'd turn back lead?"

Dawn, and the Yanks had found them again. Alistair's side felt stiff, but he drew his revolver and fired through the open threshold, aiming just below the puffs of smoke coming from the timber. Tommy Cobb stood on the other side of the doorway. Beans Kimbrough lay stretched out on the floor, revolvers in either hand, using a dead Irish boy as a redoubt.

The barrage ended, followed by a few sporadic shots, then silence. Water dripped off the roof, a frog croaked, but those natural noises were soon lost to the sounds of revolvers being reloaded and capped.

"Hell," Alistair said. "My powder's wet!"

"Here." Beans tossed him his copper flask, and Alistair busied himself loading both of his Navy Colts.

"Capt'n!" George Todd called down from the loft.

"Yes." Looking around, Alistair found Quantrill standing against the wall near a front window. They had tossed the broken old door onto the floor.

"A Yank's waving a flag of truce."

"Maybe they's surrenderin'," Henry Wilson quipped, and a smattering of laughter eased through the smoke and fog.

"Be they redlegs?" Oll Shepherd asked.

"Don't think so!" Todd called down. "Appear to be infantry. And they gots a Missouri flag."

"Infantry?" Joe Gilchrist shouted in contempt. "I ain't gettin' killed by no damned foot soldiers."

"Missouri!"

Cautiously Tommy Cobb peeked outside, the Colt in his right hand hanging by the doorjamb. "What are you Missouri boys doin'?" he yelled. "Shootin' at Missouri boys like us?"

A rifle roared, flinging Tommy back onto the floor. Screaming out an oath, he dropped the Colt onto the dirt, and fell across the dead body. Instantly Beans and Alistair had sprung toward him, grabbing his arms, dragging him away from the open door and to the wall. Another shot buzzed Alistair's neck, but then came a Yankee's shout: "Hold your fire! Hold your fire! Do not shoot until I give the order, damn you!"

Alistair could see the hole in the wall the bullet had torn out. He could also see the bloody wound in Tommy's stomach.

"Blast their hides!" Tommy shook his head. Tears rolled down his cheeks. "They've murdered me. God …" He coughed, and the crotch of his trousers darkened. "Hell's fire. Now I done wet myself."

"It's all right, Corn Cobb," Beans whispered. He shoved a folding knife into Tommy's mouth. "Bite on this."

Alistair was already trying to plug the big hole in Tommy's stomach with handkerchiefs, rags. He ripped off part of Tommy's shirt, but the blood just would not stop.

More shots rang out, but these came from inside the house, until Quantrill barked at the boys. Finally silence eased over the killing grounds.

After a moment, a Yankee called out: "We give you bush-whackers a minute to surrender! After that time, we fire this house and kill everyone as he runs out."

"They'll have a hard time getting this water-logged place a-burnin'," someone said.

"Oh," Cole Younger chimed in easily, "I allow they brung plenty of coal oil to do us right."

"Just hold your fire." Quantrill made his way over to Tommy, putting his hand on the boy's shoulder. "You did well," he said softly.

Tears filled Tommy's eyes. He spit out the knife he'd been biting on. "Thank you, Capt'n, but I reckon I'm done for."

"You are gut-shot," Quantrill said, and a coldness swept over Alistair. "There is nothing that can be done, I am loathe to say. I wish it were me, son, and not you."

"Don't say that, Capt'n." Tommy spit out bloody phlegm, tried to wipe his mouth, but his arm fell onto his thigh.

"Corn Cobb," Quantrill said, "the Yanks have us in a bind, but you can do something for us."

Alistair stared in disbelief, his mouth falling open.

"Name it, Capt'n."

"Can you walk?"

Tommy trembled, and laughed. "Well, not very far." Another cough, and gasp. "But I reckon I can travel a bit."

"I will give you a flag of truce," he said. "Walk out there. You can wear my India rubber poncho. It will hide your wound. And your revolvers."

"Tommy ..." Alistair began, but the dying farm boy shook his head.

"I can do this, Alistair." His eyes found Alistair, hard, dying, but determined.

Alistair felt himself squeezing Tommy's forearm. "I know you can," he heard himself saying, but did not, could not, look at Quantrill.

"They will meet you," Quantrill said. "When you are as close to them as you are to me, you will drop the white flag, draw your revolvers, and kill as many of those curs as you can."

Tommy spit up blood again.

"Die game," Quantrill said.

"I can do that."

"That will give us the advantage," Quantrill said. "We will then charge out, dashing to freedom, and sending as many of your murderers as we can to the pits of Hades."

Tommy looked at Alistair. "Help me up."

* * * * *

Tommy practically screamed when Beans shoved two pocket Colts into Tommy's waistband, on either side of the gaping hole. Quantrill slipped the poncho over Tommy's head, while another gave him a ramrod to carry in his left hand. They had no white shirts—nothing that could pass for white any more, anyhow—so the best they had was a faded yellow bandanna, which Cole Younger tied onto the ramrod.

"Your minute is up," the Yankee called out, "and then some!"

"We are sending a man out to discuss terms!" Quantrill yelled.

"They are no terms to discuss!" the Yank barked. "Not for bush-whacking marauders."

"We are not bushwhackers, sir," Quantrill said, "but members of the Second Arkansas Mounted Rifles. We desire to know how we will be treated upon surrender." He squeezed Tommy's shoulder. "We are honorable men, and will surrender only to honorable soldiers."

"If you got proof, we'll treat you square. Send out your man."

"Here he comes." Quantrill's smile chilled Alistair.

Before he began his walk, Tommy turned to Alistair. "You'll tell Ma and Pa how I died?" Alistair barely could nod. "Tell 'em I done my best. Tell 'em I was game."

"You're the biggest damned hero in all of Missouri, Corn Cobb," Beans said.

"You reckon?" Tommy seemed to smile.

"I know so," Quantrill said. "And your actions will give us a chance. That's all we need. One chance."

"Don't put on my tombstone that I was born in Chicago," Tommy said.

Outside, the Yankee commander demanded: "Where is your man?"

"Alistair, make sure you treat Lucy good." Tommy straightened, and stepped weakly, but proudly, outside.

CHAPTER EIGHT

"You boys let me do the talking." Frank James reined in his dun in front of the path leading to the Cobb place. "Like as not, they sha'n't have heard of Tommy's death, and Missus Cobb has always been on the peaked side. Not strong stock like most Clay County farm mothers."

"So," Beans said with a chuckle, "you don't aim to tell her how the Yanks hacked off Corn Cobb's head after they filled him with lead, stuck his noggin on a pike, and tossed the rest of his body in the burnin' shack with Joe Gilchrist, Andy Blunt, and 'em other boys who got kilt?"

Turning in his saddle, Frank James gave Beans the most chilling stare Alistair had ever seen. He could understand why Joe Gilchrist—before he'd gotten killed, by foot soldiers after all—had once said: "When Frank gets riled, a body see can see death in his eyes."

"Kimbrough," Frank said, "there are times you ain't nothing more than white trash."

Beans slumped toward his roan's withers. "Criminy, Frank," he said sheepishly, "I was just funnin'."

"No, you weren't." Frank kicked the dun into a walk, and Alistair followed. Beans mumbled something, and brought up the rear.

Corn sprouts looked promising, and the rows filled with patches of water from all the recent rain, but Alistair didn't see anyone in the fields. Likely too muddy to work right now. He could hear the thuds of an axe, and knew he'd find Mr. Cobb busy with firewood, but he was wrong.

It was Lucy.

When they rounded the woods, she sank the blade into the chopping stump, and raised her left hand to shield the sun from her eyes. Alistair spied a pepperbox hideaway pistol near the axe, and Lucy stepped closer to it before recognizing the riders. These days, company was scarce, and friendly visitors even more infrequent. Her face lit up in a grin, and Alistair's stomach almost heaved. He remembered Tommy Cobb telling everyone how he'd heard that he had been killed at Wilson's Creek. Now he came here to inform the Cobbs that their boy, Lucy's brother, was dead.

"Alistair!" Lucy sprinted from the woodshed, bare feet kicking up clods as she hurried to the dirt path. She wore a plain muslin dress, and her hair had been pinned up in a bun, but most of the blonde curls had escaped from swinging that axe. Her smile vanished, and she slid to a stop, her gaze moving from Alistair to Frank and finally to Beans.

"No." He could read her lips. Saw her wringing her hands. She turned toward the cabin and yelled: "Ma!"

That's when Alistair's heart broke.

Mrs. Cobb stepped out of the house, wiping her hands on a stained apron. Slowly she stepped off the porch, cheerful as Lucy had been for a moment, only quickly frowning. Thin as a cornstalk, she started toward them, but stopped, and had to lean against the log home for support.

Tears streamed down Lucy's face, cutting through the dirt and grime. She knew.

"Where's your pa, Miss Lucy?" Frank asked.

With a weak gesture toward the western field, Lucy turned. "He's … why yonder he comes. Musta heard y'all."

Mr. Cobb was running, his straw hat blowing off, carrying

a shotgun in both hands. He stopped, too, the double-barrel slipping from his hands and into the mud. Briefly he considered it, then left it lying there, and walked to his wife.

* * * * *

"Where did it happen?"

"The Jordan Lowe place in Jackson County," Frank told Tommy's father. "Yankees hit us at dawn Tuesday morning. Truth be told, we were in a pickle. But Tommy charged them, must have sent five or six to Glory before they killed him." He made himself face the sobbing Mrs. Cobb. "It was fast, ma'am, real quick. I don't think he felt any pain."

"He died a hero," Beans said. "Saved our bacon, sure enough. Fought like a wildcat."

With a quick nod, Mr. Cobb began fiddling with his pipe. "Well, that's good enough for me."

"But not for me!" his wife wailed. "My son is dead. *Our* son is dead. Killed." Lucy went to put her arms around her shoulders, but Mrs. Cobb flung them off. She waved a finger in Alistair's face. "Only fifteen year old, Alistair Durant. Fifteen! Had all his life ahead of him."

"That's enough," Mr. Cobb said softly at first, but, when his wife yelled something else, something no one could quite catch, he snapped. "Enough, Ermintrude. That's enough, I say!"

Her knees buckled, and Lucy caught her. "I just want ..." she sobbed as Lucy led her off the porch and into the cabin. "I just want ... my baby ... my baby ..."

The door closed, but Alistair could still hear those pitiful wails.

"Good-lookin' horses, Frank." Mr. Cobb kept messing with his pipe, spilling more tobacco onto the porch. "All you boys ride good-lookin' stock. Well, you know all about good stock, Alistair. You and your pa. Yes, sir."

Moving from the railing, Alistair took pipe and pouch from Mr.

Cobb's trembling hands. "Here, sir," he said in a voice that sounded far, far away. "Allow me, Mister Cobb."

"Good-lookin' stock. Yes, indeed." Mr. Cobb put his hand against the column. "Yankee saddles, though."

"Yankee horses," Beans said, "till we emaciated 'em. Ain't that right, Frank?"

"Emancipated," Frank corrected.

"Where about is this Jordan Lowe place?" Mr. Cobb asked. He tried to stand tall, but kept leaning against the railing. He tried to keep his lips tight. Tried to keep tears out of his eyes.

"Southwest of Independence," Frank said. "Dozen miles or so."

"Reckon Mister Lowe would let me dig up my boy? Ermintrude ... like as not, she'll want him buried alongside her ma, her pa, and our little ones that didn't make it through their second winters. She'd also want to see where he fell."

Frank had been rocking on the old chair's back legs, easy-like, but now he gripped the arms and lowered the chair back onto all fours. For a second he stared at the rough planks, then spit tobacco juice expertly between the cracks. Slowly he looked at Alistair, then let out a breath, and faced Mr. Cobb.

"I don't allow that's such a good idea, sir. Lowe abandoned the place a long while back, and ... I mean, I know it would comfort your wife and all, but, well ..." For once Frank James didn't know what to say. Suddenly he turned to Alistair again, his face pleading for help.

"It's like this here," Beans began, and Alistair quickly jumped in, afraid of what Beans would come up with.

"Yanks buried all our dead in a common grave," Alistair shot out, blending the truth with several falsehoods, making it all up on the cuff. "And burned down the buildings. The place'd been abandoned for years, like Frank said. Place like that ... well, it would just torment Missus Ermintrude. And digging up his remains ... well, sir, it's been warming up, and I don't think it would be good to ... I mean …" He fell silent. Lucy had stepped outside.

"The boys talked about it a lot, Mister Cobb," Beans said, his voice surprisingly solemn, almost like Captain Quantrill, or a preacher. "We all agreed. We'd like to be buried where we fell in battle. It's the way of a soldier, sir."

Frank and Alistair studied Beans Kimbrough long and hard. Sometimes Beans acted like doggery, but, other times, he'd surprise the hell out of a body.

"That's right, sir," Frank said. "'Then a soldier, Full of strange oaths and bearded like the pard, Jealous in honor, sudden and quick in quarrel, Seeking the bubble reputation Even in the cannon's mouth.'"

Alistair handed Mr. Cobb the pipe. Frank rose, striking a lucifer on his boot heel. After Mr. Cobb had the pipe going, he withdrew the stem, tapping the pipe on the hard railing, and said: "Reckon you be right. Frail as she is, Ermintrude wouldn't be up to a ride that far. All that way from Independence. And what you say about where a soldier fell, yes, that's the way it would be. I'll explain it to …" His voice cracked, but he quickly recovered. "No, I allow I'll just put up a headstone." He turned to Lucy for assurance. "I'll fetch the preacher. You boys stay for supper?"

"No," Frank said. "We've brought you nothing but sorrow. We'll go see our own folks."

"Be a good thing." Mr. Cobb nodded. "Your mothers'll want to see you durin' these dark days."

"Here." Frank withdrew a thick envelope from inside his waistcoat, handing the envelope to Mr. Cobb. "It's a letter from Captain Quantrill."

And some money, Alistair knew. Yankee gold. Quantrill cared little for Confederate or state script.

Leaving the pipe on the railing, Mr. Cobb took the envelope, turning it over in both dirty, thick hands, hearing the clinking of coins inside. A lone tear broke through, disappearing in his beard stubble.

"I'll read it to you, Pa," Lucy said.

His head barely bobbed. Clearing his throat, he looked again at Beans, Alistair, and Frank. "Reckon the preacher can come tomorrow afternoon if I gets word to him. You'll come to Tommy's funeral?"

"Of course," they answered in unison.

* * * * *

THOMAS BLAKE COBB
Born March 3, 1847
ASSASSINATED
by Yankees
April 15, 1862

Corn Cobb had quite the turnout. More folks kept arriving at the Cobb farm, in buckboards and farm wagons, a few on mules and horses, and many had walked. Everyone brought food. That was the Missouri way.

Alistair turned away from the wooden tombstone, knowing Lucy must have carved the words since Mr. Cobb could neither read nor write. Another wagon had pulled up, and he recognized Frank following it on that dun thoroughbred. Alistair moved from the woodshed toward the buckboard.

"Here." From her seat in the driver's box, Ma James handed him a covered dish that smelled like ham. Alistair took the platter, stepping back as Frank helped his mother down. Bearded Doc Samuel, Frank's stepfather, set the brake, and grunted as he climbed from the wagon, and tried to button his coat of black broadcloth, but promptly surrendered.

Wild-eyed Jesse, Frank's fifteen-year-old brother, leaped off the back, and Alistair helped their sister, Susan Lavenia, not quite thirteen, to the damp grass.

"Where be Ermintrude?" Ma James spit out snuff, and wiped her mouth with the back of her hand.

"Inside," Alistair said.

"Well, don't just stand there like a knot on a log!" she barked. "Get that ham inside. You-all wait out here. Jesse'd just et all the victuals good folks have brung these poor sufferin' souls. Come along, Reuben."

As Alistair and Doc Samuel followed Ma James inside, he heard Beans Kimbrough, leaning against the railing on the front porch, say underneath his breath, "Now I know why you joined up, Frank," and heard Frank snigger.

* * * * *

The McBrides were there. So was the Kennedy family. The McCoys. The Kennards. In fact, half the congregation from New Hope Baptist Church had come to pay respects to Tommy Cobb, and it was a good afternoon for a funeral. The clouds had cleared, leaving a clear blue sky.

The preacher read the Beatitudes, talked about what a fine young man Tommy Cobb had been, and what a fine life he would have lived had Yankees not cut it short. Nothing he said, though, would Alistair remember. Mrs. Cobb sat in a rocking chair, bawling throughout the whole service. Ma James spit into her small snuff cup. Menfolk stood with hats in hands, waiting for the service to end. Ladies clutched Bibles or handkerchiefs. Frank James remained away from the family plot, Remington revolver in his right hand, reins to his dun in his left, watching the path and woods for any Yankees. Beans Kimbrough was farther up, in the woods, serving as a sentry near the Centerville road.

Then Lucy Cobb, wearing a navy dress, with a black shawl over her shoulders and a black ribbon around her right arm, stepped in front of the congregation. Alistair stared as she began to sing. He never realized she had such a beautiful voice. He'd never heard this song.

We shall meet but we shall miss him.
There will be one vacant chair.
We shall linger to caress him
While we breathe our ev'ning prayer.
When one year ago we gathered,
Joy was in his mild blue eye.
Now the golden cord is severed,
And our hopes in ruin lie.

Mrs. Cobb wailed harder as Lucy began the chorus.

We shall meet, but we shall miss him.
There will be one vacant chair.
We shall linger to caress him
While we breathe our ev'ning prayer.

Ma James spit into her cup, shaking her head in apparent disgust. Cally, however, dabbed her eyes with a handkerchief and mouthed the words.

At our fireside, sad and lonely,
Often will the bosom swell
At remembrance of the story
How our noble Willie fell.
How he strove to bear the banner
Thro' the thickest of the fight
And uphold our country's honor
In the strength of manhood's might.

After the chorus, Lucy continued again.

True, they tell us wreaths of glory
Evermore will deck his brow,

But this soothes the anguish only,
Sweeping o'er our heartstrings now.
Sleep today, O early fallen,
In thy green and narrow bed.
Dirges from the pine and cypress
Mingle with the tears we shed.

A few other voices joined in as Lucy sang the chorus once more, then, breaking down, she hurried away, and ran to Alistair, who wrapped his arms around her, awkwardly, and pulled her tight.

* * * * *

After the funeral, after Mr. Cobb and Lucy managed to get some brandy down Mrs. Cobb's throat and put her to bed, they gathered in the cabin, around the tables full of food.

Ma James lowered a chicken leg and told Lucy: "That song you sang. It's a damnyankee song, ain't it?"

Cally tried to play peacemaker. "I think it's a beautiful song, Missus Zerelda."

"Damnyankee song. And secular to boot. Won't catch me allowin' a song like that played at one of my boys' funeral, God spare me the day." She dropped the greasy bone onto a tin plate.

Alistair had heard enough. "We'd best be on our way," he said, retreating. He shook Mr. Cobb's hand, paid his respects to the preacher, the McCoys, and the Jameses, and held the door open as his parents and sisters filed out.

Frank James walked to him before he left. "Week from today," he whispered. "The Jubal place. Harrisonville."

"I know. I'll be there."

"Keep a sharp eye." Frank made a beeline for his dun. "County's crawling with Yanks."

The Durants had two new mules now. Mr. McBride had even

provided Alistair's pa with a bill of sale, although those two jacks had actually been liberated after the boys had ambushed a Yankee paymaster. Alistair was helping the twins into the back of the farm wagon, when Lucy ran outside, tears streaming down her face.

"Missus Persis?" she called out.

His father had just assisted Alistair's mother into the wagon. She was putting on her bonnet, but stopped to look at Lucy.

"Yes, child?"

"Might I spend the night with y'all?" Before anyone could reply, she blurted out: "I just can't stay here tonight. I just can't. It's just for tonight."

Persis Durant pursed her lips, and looked at her husband.

"I know what you're gonna say," Lucy cried. "Family needs to be together at times like this. Ma ... she'll need me. So'll Pa. But that horrible old hag ... Zerelda ... she's stayin' here tonight. And I ..."

Alistair was afraid his mother would stare at him, but Cally sang out: "She can sleep in my bed, Ma."

"Come along, child," his mother said sweetly.

CHAPTER NINE

Back at the Tate farm, a Minié ball had plowed a furrow just below Alistair's ribs. Only a flesh wound, but it still throbbed relentlessly, and Alistair wanted to get back home, let his mother clean that ugly gash, and put a fresh bandage on him.

Last time the redlegs had paid the Durants a visit, the time they stole the horses, they'd killed all three hounds, so the farmhouse was quiet when they pulled up to the house that evening. Later, after Alistair had time to think on it, he would realize it had been too quiet. No chickens squawking. No nighthawks or bats fluttering in the gloaming. No crickets chirping. He didn't even see any fireflies.

He swung off his horse, wrapping the reins around a porch column, and gripped the harness to the mules hitched to the wagon, ready to lead them to the barn—holding the leather with both hands, away from the revolvers he had worn to see Tommy Cobb buried.

The door to the cabin opened, followed by that unmistakable metallic click of a carbine being cocked.

"Stand easy," a voice sang out, echoed by more guns being readied to fire.

One of the twins stifled a cry.

"Don't let go of that harness, young 'un," another voice said, and Alistair tightened his hold on the leather. He felt like an idiot. Frank James had warned him.

The sun had gone down, darkness quickly descending, but he could make out the silhouettes of three men approaching from the barn. Another man came around the corner of the house. Yet another popped out of the two-seat privy, standing in the doorway. That one appeared to be aiming a revolver.

"Who are you?" Alistair's father shouted. He had his hands full helping Alistair's mother from the wagon.

"Any questions will be asked by me," the man on the porch said.

"This be my property," his father said. "You'll answer to me."

"Easy, Pa," Alistair said.

"We're looking for bushwhackers," Porch Man said.

"Ain't none here!" Cally said bitterly.

"Oh, I think that's Alistair Durant holding them mules," Porch Man said.

"I'm Alistair Durant," Alistair said with a sigh. "But I'm no bushwhacker."

A match flared, and soon a lantern's wick burned, the globe being lowered, bathing the front of the house with warm light. "No bushwhacker, eh?" Porch Man laughed. "Unless my eyes deceive me, that's a bushwhacker's shirt you got on underneath that frock coat. Don't you think so, Abe?"

Abe, still standing at the privy, said: "Iffen you say so, Lieutenant." Unless Abe had eyes like a hawk, he couldn't see Alistair's face from where he stood.

"Yankee swine!" Lucy Cobb said. She stepped from the wagon, moved straight to Porch Man, and Alistair had to fight to keep his hands on the harness. He called out Lucy's name, warning her to stop, lying that everything would be fine, but she kept right on walking, eyes filled with hate. By then, however, the three men from the barn had surrounded the wagon, and one shifted his carbine to his left hand, and wrapped his right arm around Lucy's waist.

She fought like a catamount, grabbed a handful of whiskers, jerked, and the Yankee flung her to the ground, cursing while bringing the carbine to his shoulder.

"Leave her be!" Alistair shouted. He let go of the harness. The mules brayed. One started to rear up, but Cally, still in the wagon, reached across the driver's box, taking hold of the lines, calling out to the two jacks to go easy.

The twins began to cry. His father cursed the Feds. His mother sought the Almighty's deliverance.

Porch Man barked out: "No one move. This ain't what I want!"

Lucy wasn't about to stay put until Alistair shouted: "Stay there!" To his surprise, she obeyed. Oh, she didn't like it, but maybe she got a good look at that Sharps carbine aimed at her chest.

She sank back into the grass and dirt, and cursed the Federal holding the Sharps, cursed the lieutenant on the porch, cursed the other soldiers at the farm. The twins bawled, and Alistair's mother went to them, enveloping them in her arms.

"This is my farm," Able Durant said calmly. "You soldier boys ask anyone around this here county, and they'll tell you I'm no Secesh."

"Your son is," said the man who had rounded the house. Striking another match, he fired up a second lantern, which he set on the porch railing.

Cally wrapped the lines around the brake, and eased off the wagon. "You Yanks drove him to the brush," she snapped.

"Where's Quantrill?" Porch Man asked. Alistair could see his face now, but that told him little. He wore a blue kepi, and a cavalry blouse. And tall boots. So he was a regular Fed, not a redleg. The Yank who had lit the second lantern walked around, an Army Colt in his right hand, hammer at full cock. "Back up," he said.

Alistair obeyed. "You heard the lieutenant," Army Colt said. "Where's Quantrill?"

"I don't know." Which was true. Quantrill could be anywhere. In a week, he would be at the cave behind Joe Jubal's farm near Harrisonville. But this evening?

"George Todd?"

Alistair shook his head.

Porch Man stepped to the ground. "I can, and will, hang you right here."

His mother gasped, but Alistair just stared into the officer's pale eyes. He was close enough now that Alistair could see his pockmarked face, and the beginnings of a mustache and goatee.

"Tell me where Quantrill is, or even Todd, and I'll let you live. And I won't burn down this place."

Rough hands jerked down Alistair's coat. One at a time, Army Colt drew the two Navies from their holsters, and pitched the revolvers underneath the mules. Next, the Fed found the big Bowie knife, and tossed it toward the well.

"You're young to die for a murdering scoundrel like Quantrill," Porch Man said.

"I'm older than Tommy Cobb," Alistair said.

"Leave 'em be!" his mother called. "He done told you he don't know nothin'."

The twins began crying again.

"Well?" Porch Man asked.

Alistair said nothing.

With a sigh, Porch Man tilted his head toward Army Colt. "Take him inside the barn. Hang him there."

"No!" the twins and his mother cried out.

"If they move," Porch Man said, "kill them. Nits and all. You two stay here." The graybeard aiming the Sharps at Lucy nodded, and turned to point his big carbine at Alistair's father. Another soldier kept his revolver on the twins.

Lucy sprang to her feet. "I'm comin' with y'all!" she said. Tears flowed down her face. "He's my beau!"

Porch Man shrugged. "Let her come. Maybe she'll change his mind."

"If not," Army Colt said, "the barn might be a good place for her to be. Afterward." Two other Yanks sniggered with him.

With the Colt's barrel pressed against his backbone, Alistair walked toward the barn.

"Stay here," Porch Man told Privy Guard as they passed. "Keep a lookout."

Lucy ran alongside Porch Man, pleading: "You ain't gotta kill him, are you?"

"Not if he tells us where Quantrill is."

They reached the barn. Lucy helped one of the troopers open the door. "But he ain't even turned seventeen years old already. He ain't done nothin'."

"Except kill Union soldiers in a cowardly manner." Porch Man fired up another lantern. The cow kicked her stall. Army Colt holstered his revolver, found a hemp rope hanging on a nail. He uncoiled it, then tossed one end over a rafter.

"This'll do nicely, Lieutenant," he said. He didn't bother trying to fashion a hangman's knot around the rope.

"Change your mind?" Porch Man asked.

Alistair did not move, didn't even blink.

"Get on with it, Leslie," Porch Man ordered. "Tie his hands."

"Here," Alistair said, and began shedding the coat the Yanks had pulled down around his arms. "I'm no invalid."

Lucy cut loose with a pathetic wail, falling to her knees, wrapping her arms around Porch Man's waist. "Please," she begged. "Spare 'im. Spare 'im, and I'll do anything you likes."

The two Feds heading toward Alistair grinned.

Complacently Alistair put his hands behind his back. One of the guards handed his carbine to the other, withdrawing a leather cord from his trousers pocket.

"Get off me, you wench!" The lieutenant kneed Lucy in her

chest, and as she fell onto the hay, the pepperbox pistol in her hand exploded. The blaze temporarily blinded everyone in the barn, except Porch Man, who was already dead.

Bawling, the terrified milch cow kicked her stall again.

Alistair had already drawn the .31-caliber Massachusetts pocket pistol the fool Yanks hadn't found stuck near the small of his back. First, he shot the Fed holding both carbines in the stomach, then sent a ball just below the left eye of the one carrying the cord. Dropping to his knee, he tried to find Army Colt, but saw only spots from the powder flashes. Thinking he caught a glimpse of the Yank, he pulled the trigger, but heard only a click as the percussion cap misfired.

His vision cleared. He found Army Colt plain as day, leveling the pistol at Alistair's heart. Alistair dived. The revolver crashed, and Army Colt screamed, dropping his gun, his eyes rolling back. Lucy had split his skull with an axe. Quickly Alistair scooped up the Colt, pausing only long enough to put a bullet in the back of the head of the Yankee he had gut-shot. Hearing the reports of a revolver outside, he raced into the darkness.

By then, the gunfire had ceased. He heard nothing other than the ringing in his ears. Cally and Able Durant ran toward him. Alistair lowered his revolver, looking beyond them. His father and sister stopped, then Alistair turned, saw Lucy stepping out of the barn.

"You all right, Son?" his father asked.

"Yeah."

"Alistair!" Beans Kimbrough called from the porch.

"I'm all right." He breathed a little easier.

Beans had listened to Frank James, but Beans was always cautious, had insisted on hanging back, cutting through the woods to make sure everything was fine at the Durant farm.

Alistair moved past his father, warning him and his sister: "Y'all stay out of the barn. We'll clean things up. But if y'all can take care of Lucy …"

He moved past the privy, glimpsing the dead Yankee leaning

against the door. It was too dark to see much about the dead man's body, which was just fine with Alistair.

His mother had picked up the twins, and rushed them inside. Candles flickered through the window. His mother, trying to calm down the little ones, started a hymn, managing only a few words before having to suck in deep breaths and exhale, then trying again, her voice cracking.

Beans flung one corpse into the back of the wagon. Alistair slid the Army Colt by the dead man's boots, and helped Beans with the other dead man.

His father stopped by the wagon, staring, his eyes blank as Cally, her arm around Lucy's shoulder, helped her into the cabin.

"I'm sorry this had to happen," Alistair said.

"It ain't …" His father looked away. "Ain't your … fault."

"We'll take the bodies away from here, sir," Beans said. "Dump 'em at the ferry." He peered toward the fields, the woods, the creekbed, although it was too dark now to see much of anything. "Must have horses around here somewhere. We'll fetch 'em up, too. I know a guy up by the mill who ain't particular what kind of horses and tack he buys. So when Yankees come 'round here askin' questions, you just say you ain't never seen no Yanks. Not tonight. Not ever. You ain't seen your son, neither."

Without a word, Able Durant turned, quickly disappearing inside the house. The twins sobbed. Candles flickered. Lucy groaned. His mother tried to sing. His sister whispered.

"I'll fetch the other bodies," Beans said. "They all dead?"

Alistair could barely nod.

"Take that lantern over yonder. See if you can find their mounts. Must be hid in the woods or somewheres. We gots to get rid of anything the Yanks brung here."

Dumbly Alistair nodded. Suddenly he realized that his side no longer throbbed. He felt no pain. No remorse, no sickness or shame, no regret. He feared, however, that he was beginning to feel nothing.

Just like Beans Kimbrough.

Already Beans sat in the wagon, grabbing the reins, releasing the brake, moving the vehicle toward the privy to pick up the dead man there. "Like I say, we'll dump the bodies far from here. At the ferry, I think. And we'll ride on."

Ride on. Alistair sighed. *Ride on.*

After tonight, he could never return home.

CHAPTER TEN

The world passed by in a whirlwind.

Less than a week after they buried Tommy Cobb, President Jefferson Davis signed into Confederate law the "Partisan Ranger Act of 1862," giving guerrillas like Quantrill and his men some legitimacy. Yankees, of course, usually still executed captured irregulars on the spot.

Quantrill did the same with Feds. Well, he might hold a regular soldier hostage, maybe for barter, trying to exchange a prisoner. But jayhawker or redleg? They never lived long. Like the time after they captured ten of Jennison's raiders. One of the Kansans had an Enfield rifle, so sixteen-year-old Dill McCoy made the prisoners stand close together in a straight line, just to see how many bodies an Enfield's bullet could shoot through. The answer? Eight. Arch Clements shot the other two in the head with his revolver.

They robbed mail carriers, ambushed Yankee patrols. They captured a steamboat, the *Little Blue*, which happened to be carrying forty sick Yanks. That turned into a regular jollification after Jim Cummins called out: "Hey, Capt'n, let's make 'em walk the plank."

So they fashioned a plank, and prodded those who could walk to step over the side and into the river. Those too sick to stand were flung overboard like fish too small for frying. When the doctors protested, the boys made those white-frocked sawbones step into the river, too. Criminy, it was only five feet deep or thereabouts. Wasn't like they were drowning anybody, and Beans Kimbrough helped fish one sick Fed out of the river when they realized the fool couldn't swim. After such a grand time, the boys didn't even torch the side-wheeler.

Usually things weren't so fun.

In July, they tangled with troops from the First Iowa and Seventh Missouri. That little fracas had been almost like a real fight, not an ambush. Until Quantrill ordered the boys to retreat into a ravine, and the Yanks followed.

Summer had turned savagely hot, relentlessly humid. Briars and branches scratched Alistair's face, knocked his hat off as he slid six feet down the bank. A bullet singed his long locks. He turned, fired, but all he hit was the trunk of an oak. A soldier landed to his right. Their eyes met, and the Fed raised a saber, but only wedged the blade between two limbs. Alistair shot him in the head, pulled himself into a crouch, and moved through the brush.

"Get down!" Frank James yelled from up ahead, and Alistair dropped flat.

A volley cracked behind him, Minié balls whistled over his head, thudded into trees, spanged off rocks. He scrambled to his feet as the Feds reloaded. Took shelter behind a slab of rock. Heard a Yankee scream: "Charge!"

A mass of bluecoats appeared in the brush, bayonets catching the rays of sunlight that crept through the thick overgrowth deep in the ravine.

"Look at 'em all!" someone shouted. "Why ...?" His words were lost in a battery of revolver shots.

Badly wounded, Ezra Moore, shot off his horse, was trying to crawl away, and a bluecoat plunged a long bayonet through the small of his back. Ezra cried out in agony, and the Yank stuck him again. When the trooper pulled out that big blade, Ezra rolled over on his back, and sent a bullet in the trooper's stomach. As he fell, the Yank jammed the bayonet in Ezra's heart, and dropped dead on a log to Ezra's left.

A Rebel yell filled the ravine, echoing off the rocks, through the brush. The boys met the charging Yanks in one savage affair.

Alistair rose to his feet, felt the Navy buck in his hand, and suddenly he was screaming, too, emptying one .36, then another, smashing a bluecoat's face with the walnut butt. He found his Bowie, slashed, hacked. Blood splashed across his face, and he could taste it—warm, sticky, salty. He rammed the blade through a leather belt, heard a pitiful wail.

In minutes, the Federals were running back, climbing out of the ravine, leaving the dead and dying. An eerie stillness filled the woods.

Alistair sank onto his buttocks, wiping his face with a bandanna. A canteen lay beside him, and he picked it up, pulled out the cork, and drank greedily.

"God A'mighty!" He coughed up the whiskey, turned to his side, and gagged.

"What's the matter?" George Todd asked him. "Too damned bloody for you?"

Alistair pitched the canteen to the rocks. "That ain't water," he said. "It's forty-rod."

"Well, hell's bells, boy." Todd laughed and grabbed the canteen, taking a long pull, then smiling after wiping his lips with the back of his hand.

"Whiskey!" Clell Miller laughed. "That's how come 'em blue-belly dogs fight so hard."

Alistair pushed himself up.

Bill Anderson kneeled next to a dead Yank, working his skinning knife. The scalp popped as Anderson jerked, then eased the bloody trophy into a pocket on his bushwhacker's shirt.

"How many did you get this time, Bill?" Todd called out.

"Only three," Anderson answered grimly, and began tying knots in the silk cord he carried.

Looking down, Alistair realized he was sitting on a corpse. Sightless eyes stared up at him, the mouth open in a terrifying but silent scream, and Alistair vomited, pushed himself up, dropping the knife onto the body.

"Too much whiskey, kid?" Arch Clements snorted.

"Too much blood," George Todd said.

"Leave him be." It was Cole Younger, and few of the boys were dumb enough to disobey Cole Younger. The big man picked up one of Alistair's Navy Colts, slid it into the holster, turned Alistair around, and gave him a gentle nudge.

"Yanks'll be regroupin'," Younger said. "We best ride."

"Let 'em come," Anderson said. "I'll kill thirty more today."

"We ride!" Quantrill yelled. "Mount up."

Alistair took in a deep breath, saw the bloody rag wrapped around the captain's thigh. The former schoolteacher grimaced as Beans Kimbrough helped him into the saddle. Gripping the reins, Beans led horse and rider up the steep slopes out of the ravine.

Alistair and Cole stepped over bodies—bushwhackers and Feds—some lying atop each other. Behind him came the occasional shot of one of the boys finishing off a dying soldier. Alistair stopped, stared at two boys, maybe his age, locked together in death.

"God," he said.

"Keep movin', Durant." Cole pushed him toward the tethered horses.

"Doesn't this bother you, Cole?" Alistair asked.

"Boy, Yanks murdered my pa," Cole answered. "Dumped his body in a bar ditch. Drove me to the brush just like they done you. They brung the wrath of God upon themselves."

He had called Alistair *boy*. Cole Younger was eighteen, only a year older than Alistair, whose seventeenth birthday had come and gone without notice. Bill Anderson was in his early twenties, George Todd maybe around the same. Frank James, nineteen. Beans Kimbrough, seventeen. Jim Cummins looked even younger than Alistair. By thunder, Quantrill himself couldn't be older than twenty-five.

Cole lifted Alistair's left boot into the stirrup, then pushed him, as Alistair grabbed mane and rein, into the saddle. Alistair stared down into the Cole's beard-stubbled face.

Cole Younger looked over the cantle at Anderson, Todd, and the others, gathering whiskey-filled canteens, revolvers, wallets, and scalps. Finally his blue eyes locked on Alistair.

"But if it don't bother you, boy ..."—Alistair could see the blood on Cole's brow and cheeks, his face hard, but those pale eyes red rimmed from sweat and gunpowder, and, maybe, just maybe, some remorse and pity—"then you're already dead. Like Todd, Anderson, maybe even the capt'n hisself."

* * * * *

They ambushed more mails, more Yankee patrols. They hanged three redlegs under a bridge. They raided Independence. They met up with some regular Confederate officer at a farm west of Lone Jack, where the colonel made everything official, mustering Quantrill and the boys into the Confederate Army. As Partisan Rangers.

"This mean we get paid?" Dill McCoy asked.

"In Confederate script," a gray-coated captain said with a grin. "Whenever the paymaster happens by."

"We can do better than that," Chris Kennard said.

"But don't worry," George Todd said, "the bluebellies will still hang us anyway."

"Not iffen we die game," Beans Kimbrough said.

Quantrill was officially elected captain. The boys voted William Haller as first lieutenant, which riled George Todd considerable. Todd had been voted second lieutenant, and William Gregg third lieutenant. Within minutes after the announcement, Frank James and Oll Shepherd were separating Todd and Haller. A regular Confederate sergeant had to knock a pistol out of Todd's hand.

"Captain!" the colonel shouted. "Arrest those two officers."

"I don't think so, Colonel," Quantrill said mildly.

The officer's face flushed with anger, his hands balled into fists, and he stood there shaking. For a moment, Alistair thought there might be a fight between the regular army and the boys, but the bearded colonel let out a long breath, and, with contempt, said: "Your men lack discipline."

Quantrill, still favoring his left leg, grinned. "But they fight, Colonel. They fight like the devil himself."

Indeed, they fought. At Lone Jack. On the Little Blue. On lonely roads. At once prosperous farms. They even covered the rear as the Confederate Army retreated south toward Arkansas to join up with General Jo Shelby. Which was fine with the boys. They never cared much for fighting with the regular army anyway. Too many orders. Not enough killing.

They hid in the ravines, in the thickets, in caves. They raided Olathe, Kansas, and murdered Yankee prisoners. Payback for the execution of one of the boys at Fort Leavenworth.

Still, every now and then, Frank James, Dill McCoy, Beans, or Alistair would ride to Watkins Mill. Trying to find out about Alistair's or Frank's family, catch up on news, and, if only briefly, touch humanity.

On the first week of November, Beans Kimbrough rode into camp at Red Bridge near the Kansas border. He had been gone three weeks, so long some of the boys were taking bets on whether he'd been captured and killed.

"It pains me to see you alive, Beans," Henry Wilson said lightly. "You done cost me a five-shot Bulldog revolver."

Alistair started to rise from the campfire, but the look on Beans' face caused him to slip back to the ground. He fingered the rim of his coffee cup.

Beans stepped near the fire, easing his saddlebags to the ground, and sliding into a seat on the log next to Frank James, who asked: "How are things back home?"

"Not so good," Beans said. "Yanks have arrested some womenfolk."

Cole Younger rose angrily. "What in tarnation for?"

"Because they're Yanks!" Bill Anderson roared.

"Your sisters are among them, Bill," Beans said.

The look flashing through Anderson's eyes tied Alistair's stomach in knots. Slowly Anderson began to stand, his hands resting on the butts of his revolvers.

"Sit down, Bill." Quantrill had walked from his tent to the fire.

"Be damned if I will."

"You are already damned, Bill. Sit, I say." Quantrill's jaw jutted toward Beans. "What is this, Beans?"

So Beans explained. Yanks had arrested several sisters of men known, or merely suspected, to have ridden with Quantrill. Called them spies. Had them locked up in an old building on Grand Avenue in Kansas City that they'd converted into a women's prison. Josephine, Jennie, and Mary Anderson—"Jennie ain't but ten years old!" Bill Anderson roared—John McCorkle's sister and sister-in-law. A bunch of others. Slowly Beans turned to Alistair. "Cally's in there with them," he said softly. "So's Lucy."

A coldness swept over Alistair, almost paralyzing him.

"They wage war now on our women!" Quantrill shook his head, and let out a bitter laugh. "Well, I shall write a letter of protest to General Ewing."

"I say, Capt'n," Bill Anderson said, his voice sinister, "that we mount up right now and ride to Kansas City. We free our women. We kill every Yankee, every Unionist ..."

"You do that, Bill, and you'll get all those girls kilt." For once, even George Todd sided with Captain Quantrill. Even rarer, Bill Anderson listened.

"I read in the *Times*, Alistair, that they suspect you was involved in them horse soldiers getting kilt," Beans said, changing the subject, which brought everyone, even Quantrill, up short. They merely stared. "Thought I had fixed that by dumpin' them bodies by the ferry," Beans added.

Alistair reached for the coffee pot, just to do something. Maybe Beans had tried to hide all the evidence at the farm, but considering the tempers of Lucy Cobb and Cally Durant, and the Yankee presence in this part of Missouri, well, it was just a matter of time before those girls stirred up trouble.

"But I think I fixed things, pard." Squatting, Beans opened one of the bags, and pulled out a tattered *St. Louis Republican*. He started to hand the newspaper to Alistair, but quickly decided to give it to Captain Quantrill, pointing to a column on the second page.

Quantrill read, silently at first, then aloud, eyes flashing, voice rising like a regular Thespian treading the boards.

I read in the *Star* that Federal authorities have arrested Lucy Cobb and Cally Durant for suspicion of aiding and abetting Captain Quantrill's alleged murder of several soldiers of the First Iowa Cavalry in Clay County in April.

It shames me that two innocent girls in their teens could be placed in harm's way, as it should shame General Ewing and even President Abraham Lincoln. It makes me laugh that Federal soldiers are so ignorant they blame a young farmer named Alistair Durant—brother of Cally, and betrothed to Miss Cobb …

Here, the campfire echoed with snickers. Jim Cummins punched Alistair's arm and said: "You ain't the greenhorn I taken your fer, boy. Betrothed! Ha!"

"Silence," Quantrill ordered, and continued to read.

… for assisting in the deaths of Yankee vermin who make war on innocent farmers.

Ask anyone in Clay County, and they will swear on a Bible that Mr. Able Durant is a peaceful farmer. He doesn't even own a Negro slave to help out around his farm, but relies on the sweat of his own person, and that of his lone son.

That lone son has been forced into "outlawry" by murdering jayhawkers and redlegs, men who disgrace even Union officials.

Let me make a confession here and now. The Durant family is innocent. I, and I alone, killed those Iowa horse soldiers at the ferry on the Missouri River betwixt Liberty and Lexington. Every single one died at my hand, several after they surrendered, but, like the Union Army, I take no prisoners. I take lives. And I will kill many more.

Remember my name, and remember it well. And never, ever forget Osceola!

> Benedict "Beans" Kimbrough
> Partisan Ranger
> Capt. William Quantrill,
> Commanding

Around the campfire, the boys cheered, slapping Beans' back, while Quantrill absently handed the paper to someone who wanted to see it for himself.

"You wrote that?" Quantrill shook his head.

Beans laughed. "By myself."

"You ain't the ignorant son-of-a-bitch I taken you for," George Todd said.

"I don't use rough language around my mama."

Frank James handed Beans a bottle of rye, and, after taking a long pull, Beans grinned and continued. "I don't cuss in front of a preacher. But when I'm around rough people ..." Laughing, he tossed the bottle to Quantrill.

Raising a clay jug overhead, Oll Shepherd cheered.

"Shut up!" Alistair shot to his feet. He hadn't meant to yell, but this was all wrong. "You damned fool." Alistair waved a finger in Beans' face, who merely smiled, and snatched the jug from Shepherd's grip. "Yanks didn't even know who you were," Alistair said. "Now you've given them your name."

Beans' green eyes became ice. "It is a name they will well remember, too, Alistair Durant. I aim to make it known all across Kansas and Missouri."

"Hear, hear!" Chris Kennard thundered.

"You …" Alistair couldn't find the words.

"Quiet, Mister Durant," Quantrill said. He sipped from the bottle, passed it to Lieutenant Haller, and laughed. "You are an intelligent man, Mister Kimbrough," Quantrill continued. "And I have need of intelligent men. You and Mister Durant will come with me. Lieutenant Haller, you shall be in charge during my absence."

"Where be you goin'?" Todd roared.

"To Richmond," Quantrill replied.

RICHMOND

CHAPTER ELEVEN

"There." Quantrill adjusted the blue and white polka dot cravat around Alistair's neck, tugged on the paper collar that scratched his freshly shaved neck, and stepped back. The captain's blue eyes sparkled, until he spotted a speck of dust, which he quickly brushed off the gray frock coat.

Quantrill's head started to bob, but suddenly he doubled over in laughter. The instant he managed to lift his head, his composure left him again, and he guffawed uncontrollably, until, wiping the tears from his eyes, he managed to hurry to the chest of drawers in the hotel room. Atop the chest rested a decanter of brandy. Quantrill filled a cordial, and drank.

"You ..." Making the mistake of facing Alistair, he exploded in laughter once more.

By that time, Alistair's ears began reddening. He glanced at Beans Kimbrough, who had stopped brushing his gaiters, but merely shrugged.

"You ... oh, my!" Finally Quantrill set down the empty cordial, dabbing his eyes with a silk handkerchief. "You look like the proverbial cat who has eaten the canary."

"I'm not used to all this foofaraw." Alistair picked up the

receipt lying on the divan, and flashed it at Quantrill. "And what these Virginians charge for duds is obscene."

Quantrill walked toward him, suddenly looking sympathetic. He cut a dashing figure. Upon arriving in the Confederate capital last week, they had stopped at a tailor's shop on Fourteenth Street. Now, Quantrill wore light blue trousers with a yellow stripe up the seams, tucked inside gleaming black boots that came up to his knees. Underneath his dark gray, double-breasted shell jacket with a high yellow collar and the three bars identifying his rank of captain, he wore a blue silk shirt, paper collar, and black tie. Around his waist was a leather belt, a new LeMat revolver holstered on his left hip, butt forward, and a saber sheathed on his left. Yellow doeskin gauntlets and a yellow-trimmed gray kepi lay near the decanter.

For some reason, Quantrill had stopped at another tailor to fashion the clothes Alistair and Beans picked up that morning. Not military, but civilian attire. Broadcloth pants, gaiters for Beans but boots for Alistair, formal coats, waistcoats, the finest shirts you could find in Richmond these days. When Beans had tried to sneak a pocket pistol into his frock coat, Quantrill had objected, saying that one did not call on the kings of the Confederacy with hideaway guns.

Beans looked the part of a Virginia nobleman, but Alistair had grown up on a hard-scrabble farm. Never had he owned clothes like this. When he went to church, he'd wear a black string tie and worn frock coat, a hand-me-down from his father. He started to run a finger around the starched paper collar, which choked him like a gallows noose.

Gently Quantrill gripped Alistair's shoulders, and guided him toward the full-length mirror hanging near the bed.

"You, sir, are a dashing young man," Quantrill spoke smoothly. "The Richmond gentry will envy you. All the ladies will cast looks in your direction. Their looks will be discrete, but their thoughts shall lack any proper decorum."

They had splurged on hot baths, close shaves, and five-course meals in the best restaurants Richmond had to offer. The only thing Beans and Alistair would not relent to was getting their locks shorn. Alistair's hair fell past his shoulders, and Beans' was even longer.

"We cut our hair," Beans had reminded the captain, "after we've won, when redlegs and Yankees are burnin' in hell."

Quantrill had not argued. In Missouri, such was the code of bushwhackers.

"Seems that money would've been better spent," Alistair mumbled, "on powder and lead." Still, he picked up the silk hat and topped his head with it, tilting it slightly.

"You are not a rake, Alistair." Quantrill set the hat at a more proper angle.

Seeing Quantrill's grin in the mirror, Alistair couldn't help himself. A smile stretched across his face. He'd give a bushel of corn if his parents, or Lucy Cobb, could see him now.

"Come." Quantrill spun, long strides carrying him to the chest of drawers, where he fetched gauntlet and kepi. "Let us call on President Davis."

* * * * *

Despite seven days in Richmond, Alistair yet remained in awe. Brick, wooden, and stone buildings seemed to stretch on forever. Grain mills, ironworks, factories, warehouses, riverboats, gunboats, tanning yards, slaves, soldiers, civilians. The crisp December air felt so heavy with smoke, he found it hard to breathe. Or maybe it was just because he'd never seen so many people crowding the streets.

The bellman at the hotel had said Richmond had boasted a population of nigh forty thousand before the war. By now, that had doubled. Some suspected that it would soon triple. Which was why they were lucky even to find a room at a decent hotel.

"I should warn you not to tarry in the city streets after dark," the bellman had warned Quantrill. "Undesirables have turned our fair city into a Sodom. Juveniles will rob you for the coin in your pocket. Gentlemen are not safe."

Quantrill had thanked the man and planted a coin in his palm. Out of earshot, he had laughed, elbowing Beans in the side. "Do you think that old boy could survive a week in Cass County?"

Still, Alistair thought Quantrill remained alert as they wove through the throng. He clutched an ivory-tipped cane tightly in his right hand, gripping the handle of his saber with his left.

Soon, Alistair relaxed. No criminal would try to rob them, not in broad daylight, not with ten thousand people moving, or trying to move, in the town center. Most white men hurried about like ants, too busy to notice him in his new duds. Even those ladies with their parasols and fine dresses did not give him much attention.

He also noticed the soldiers. Scores of them, many heavily bandaged, several jaundiced, some on crutches with their pants legs pinned up above their knees—or where their knees once had been.

One soldier laughed at Alistair's stare, and snorted: "You shoulda been here directly after Seven Days, boy. City was filled with us invalids."

His companion planted a hand on the cripple's shoulder. "Jeb here had both limbs in May." He raised his other hand, revealing a white-wrapped stump. "And I had both hands."

Still another cried out: "Walk up to Chimborazo, fellas! You'll see what it's really like to be a soldier."

And yet another: "He's too yellow to fight. Look at those habiliments."

Beans stopped, turned, and started to say, "I'll tell you about Osceola. Better yet, I'll kick your—" but Quantrill shoved him forward, almost knocking over an elderly man carrying a brown sack and a newspaper. "Keep moving," Quantrill said angrily. "Do not engage them. And act like a darky. Do not look anyone in the eye."

With a curse, Beans kept up pace.

* * * * *

The Confederate Capitol came straight out of a storybook about Rome. Before the war, it had been the state capitol, designed in part by Thomas Jefferson.

Quantrill hurried up the marble steps, dodging the myriad black slaves working for the War Department.

An hour later, Alistair found himself in a spartan room, extending his hand to the Confederate Secretary of War.

"And this," Quantrill said, "is my other adjutant, Beans ... uh, well ..." A sheepish laugh escaped, and he stepped back, shaking his head. "Beans, my stalwart comrade, I believe that your true name escapes me."

"Benedict, Mister Secretary." Beans shook hands. "But I prefer Beans."

James A. Seddon looked neither amused nor impressed. He looked perturbed, as if his day had been ruined by this meeting with a captain named Quantrill and two teenage boys in handsome suits.

"Beans Kimbrough?" A man between forty and fifty, Seddon was balding on top with long graying hair on the sides, a high forehead, mustache and goatee, massive eyebrows, and angry eyes. His coat was out of fashion, as was his vest, and, after shaking Beans' hand, he moved back behind his desk, and glanced at a stack of newspapers. He shuffled through two, glanced at the third, and peered at Beans. "Beans Kimbrough?" he repeated.

"Yes, sir." Beans looked as big a fool as Alistair.

Quantrill cleared his throat, his face angry, and, after a moment of silence, Seddon absently gestured at the high-backed chairs in front of his desk.

"I regret to say that President Davis cannot meet with you today, and has asked me to serve as his liaison." Seddon sank into his chair, started to open a cigar box, changed his mind, and leaned back in the chair. Grouchily he leaned forward, his chair squeaking, and glanced at a note on his desk top, then leaned back. "You understand that Congress passed the Partisan Ranger

Act last spring, and President Davis has signed it into law?"

"Of course." Handing Alistair his walking cane, Quantrill removed his gauntlets, sticking them under his left arm with his kepi. "And, you, I suspect, understand that Federal authorities refuse to treat us, when captured, with the respect due prisoners of war."

"That ..."—Seddon leaned back in his chair, looking at the newspapers—"cuts both ways, according to our reports from Missouri."

"My lieutenants here, Kimbrough and Durant, must wear civilian attire in battle, and everywhere." Quantrill nodded in the boys' direction.

Alistair and Beans shot each other curious glances, thinking the same thing. Lieutenants? Haller, Todd, Bill Gregg were lieutenants. Beans and Alistair held no rank, unless you called them privates, which none of the boys ever did.

"Is it uniforms you seek, Captain?"

"Far from it. In battle, we don bushwhacker shirts. Ladies of Missouri have embroidered them, decorated them. They are the envy of those soldiers in butternut and gray."

"And sometimes," Seddon said, "from reports out of Missouri, you wear the uniforms of Federal soldiers."

Quantrill grinned. "Surprise is a most efficient tactic, Mister Secretary."

"What is it that you wish, Captain Quantrill?" Seddon turned blunt as a sledgehammer.

"I would like to recruit a regiment. I would like a commission as colonel. I would like to lead a campaign in Missouri and Kansas. I would like to win this war in the West, Mister Secretary. It must be won there. You are not winning it here, sir."

Alistair tried to swallow, but couldn't summon up enough spit. Quantrill could be blunt himself.

"Captain Quantrill, we drove the Federals out this summer," Seddon said, "when they thought they would wave the Stars and

Stripes over Richmond for Independence Day. At Manassas, once more this summer, we again defeated that army, and, not two weeks back, General Lee crushed Burnside at Fredericksburg, a scant sixty miles north of here. This autumn, we earned a hard-fought victory in Maryland at Sharpsburg. In a short while, the Northern states will force President Lincoln and his Congress to sue us for peace. Yet you say we are not winning the war, Captain?"

Quantrill smiled. "You call Sharpsburg a victory, Mister Secretary?"

"Indeed." Indignation flashed in Seddon's eyes.

"Victories such as that will cost you this war, sir. And how many men did you lose at Fredericksburg, sir?" Seddon didn't answer. "The North can afford more casualties than your gallant General Lee, sir. Look West, my good man. Vicksburg is in trouble. You had General Grant decimated at Shiloh this spring, but let victory slip away. Fort Donelson has fallen. The Mississippi River is in danger of being in Yankee hands. The Union blockade is strong. Do you know how much it cost my adjutants and myself merely to eat breakfast this morning? I have rarely seen a bakery open past ten in the morning, and what they charge for a loaf of bread is criminal. The grain mills here fall eerily silent. This once grand city overflows with the destitute. Besides, England has not recognized your ... our government."

"In time."

"Time is short."

Seddon shifted uncomfortably in his seat. "I warrant that you have a plan of battle, Captain?"

"Indeed, Mister Secretary. This Secession, this revolution, this whatever you feel it should be called, whatever history will call it ... well, to win, to conquer, this must be done with violence."

"Sharpsburg was no picnic, sir."

"Nor was it the Confederate victory you claim, Mister Secretary." When Seddon began to push himself to the floor, Quantrill held out his right hand. "Hear me out, sir. I have traveled at my own expense, risked my own life and the lives of these two young

Missourians, to try to help my men, and to try to help our cause, sir. You owe me that much, do not you think?"

"Speak your piece, Captain."

"War is violent. War is vindictive. Men must be killed."

"I still wait to hear your plan of battle." He had dropped the *sir* and the *captain*.

"It is this … I would wage such a war to make surrender forever impossible. I would cover the Confederate armies with blood. I would invade. I would reward audacity, not temerity. I would exterminate." Here his voice raised. "Exterminate by indiscriminate massacre." He walked as he spoke, tossing kepi and gauntlets to Beans, and reached Seddon's desk. His hands gripped the edge, and he leaned forward. Seddon's face paled. "I would win the independence of our people, my people, or I would find them graves."

Silence filled the room. Even the clock could not be heard.

"What of prisoners?" Seddon's voice trembled.

Smiling, Quantrill released his grip on the desk and laughed. "There would be no prisoners. I do not surrender. I do not panic. What I do, and what I do well, Mister Secretary, is hate. If you would leave this civilized city, I could show you how easy it is to hate when one lives in Missouri.

"I am hunted, but I hunt my hunters. I am outlawed, but I outlaw my enemies. They have made my name blacker than two dozen devils, but I will blacken the names and the bodies of men like Senator James Lane and Doc Jennison. My plan, sir? It is simple. Meet torch with torch, pillage with pillage, slaughter with slaughter, subjugation with extermination. I will lay Kansas to waste. That, Mister Secretary, is how you win a war." He retrieved his gauntlets and kepi from Beans, setting the cap on his head, pulling on his gloves, and, turning, he snapped to attention and saluted.

"Come along, lads." He grabbed his cane from Alistair's hand. "I dare say that Secretary Seddon has heard enough for one afternoon."

CHAPTER TWELVE

Back in the hotel room, they sat in silence, Quantrill staring out the open window despite the cold, watching snow accumulate on the sill, on the sidewalks below. Beans Kimbrough rested on the divan, holding a copy of W. H. Ainsworth's *The Combat of the Thirty*. Alistair had just turned the page on George Eliot's *The Mill on the Floss*, but, if anyone had asked him what he had just read, he couldn't have even guessed.

The decanter on the chest of drawers had been emptied, but a street vendor had remedied that. Quantrill filled a stein with the last of the first bottle, which he tossed toward a brass cuspidor, but missed.

"I heard on the streets this evening that another battle is being engaged somewhere in Tennessee, south of Nashville, I believe. I had hoped to return to Missouri via Tennessee."

Quantrill's voice sounded lonely, distant, cold as the weather outside. He had not spoken much since leaving the War Department, and it surprised Beans and Alistair, who quickly closed the books they hadn't really been reading.

"Mayhap we shall journey through Kentucky." Quantrill sipped his liquor. He kept staring outside.

"Maybe you could see your folks," Beans offered. "Your ma and pa."

Quantrill spun so quickly, he splashed bourbon on the drapes. "My father!" The stein slammed on the table beside him. "My father burns in perdition's hottest flames, or so is my fervent desire. A brute, a drunkard, a rapscallion with an iron hand, it was a beautiful day in Dover, Ohio, when consumption claimed his sorry life."

Beans eyed Alistair, then, before Alistair could warn him not to ask, said: "Thought you said you hailed from Kentucky."

Quantrill hadn't heard. With a snigger, he sipped bourbon, spilling more down his unbuttoned shell jacket. "Would have been beautiful, except for the poverty he left us in. My ma, without a penny to her name or brain in her head, and Mary my sister, she and that curved spine. A cripple, and a cripple is no help when you are dirt poor." Another laugh and another drink. "Perhaps it was for the best. I had to go earn money. So west I went. Yes, here's to you, Pa, for dying. Wish you had done it sooner." He mockingly toasted the mirror. This time, he drained the stein. "But, Father, you did teach me a few things, reprobate and swindler that you were. Yes." He uncorked the second and last bottle. "Yes, to Missouri we must return. George Todd is not one to be trusted with command for too long. Pack. We leave tomorrow."

"Tomorrow?" Alistair said uneasily.

"Yes, confound it. Tomorrow. A battle is being fought in Tennessee, but a war is being waged in Missouri. We must return to the fight."

Alistair remembered the wounded soldiers scattered across the vast city of Richmond. A war, a brutal war, was being fought here, too.

"I thought ..." Here, he stumbled. Quantrill suddenly appeared sober, but Alistair knew that to be far from the case. Yet his eyes chilled him, held him.

"You thought what?"

"Well, the secretary ... Seddon, he hasn't answered ..."

"He sha'n't respond." Quantrill drank greedily. "Did you see the look he gave me." Moving unsteadily and laughing, Quantrill fetched a rolled newspaper from the pocket of his greatcoat. "Oh,

I forgot. You remember how Seddon appeared to recognize your name, Beans." He dropped the wet *Dispatch* in Alistair's lap, instead of Beans', and retreated to the bottle.

Beans came off the divan to look over Alistair's shoulder. The *Dispatch* had reprinted Beans' letter published in the St. Louis *Republican*.

"They shall remember your name, Beans Kimbrough," Quantrill said, laughing as he splashed bourbon into his stein. "And remember it well."

Beans turned into a lamb, straightening, blurting out: "I'm sorry, sir. If that letter has cost you ..."

"It cost me nothing, Kimbrough." Quantrill drank. "Wars are not won or lost by words in newspapers, either, Beans. No, that is not why Seddon will refuse to see me again, refuse to hear me out, or grant any request." Another swig. "Did you see how he looked at me?"

Staring out the window, he spoke in a voice so low, Alistair could just barely make out the words.

"He thinks me mad. Yet, I will show him madness. They think there are rules of war that must be followed, but the only rule there is ... is to kill your enemy, kill his friends, kill his cattle, kill his pigs, kill his dignity." He looked up, ran his fingers through his hair, tried not to stagger, but failed, stepping toward Alistair and Beans, but stopping a few feet from the boys, swaying. "You know why I did this, don't you, boys? I did it for you. I care not for the commission as a colonel. I just want you to be treated humanely if, God forbid, you should ever be captured by our bloodthirsty enemy. Not for me. I have no intention of surrendering. But you ... You see? That's why we came here. For you."

Beans said: "Thank you, Captain."

"It's *colonel*!" Quantrill stood erect, rigid. "I care not a whit what James Seddon says. From here on out, you shall address me as colonel. I deserve that rank." After another drink, he refilled the stein.

"Colonel," Alistair said uneasily, but he had to say something, get one point across no matter how drunk Quantrill was getting. "I thought maybe ... well ... those girls ... the ones the Yanks have arrested and are holding in that prison in Kansas City?"

"What of them?"

"Maybe President Davis ... maybe Secretary Seddon ... I thought maybe we came here to do something about them? For them?"

"Women?" Quantrill had taken both stein and bottle back to the window to resume staring into the blackness of night and the whiteness of snow. "Do something for women? Like my mother, who nags for money because she has no sense whatsoever? 'Willie, please, I beg of you, we are so poor, any copper or silver would do ... gold if you have it.' And while I was starving in the Colorado and Utah Territories, hard and scaly times to be sure, or while I was trying to teach Kansas sodbusters how to read and write, while I knew the true meaning of dire straits ... did my mother, my brother, my invalid sister give me anything?" He paused and pushed back the curtain, grinning. "Why, there's a lovely lass now. Alone at this time of night. I dare say, she must not have heard about the villainy running amok in this fair city."

He placed the stein on the table, grabbed his kepi, forgetting greatcoat and gauntlets, and hurried to the door, buttoning his shell jacket as he strode across the room.

The door closed, and Alistair and Beans looked at each other, struck dumb. A gust of wind brought Alistair to his feet, and he went to close the window.

"Whiskey got to him tonight," he said, staring outside. He could see no lass, no Quantrill, could see nothing but the occasional mule-drawn hack cutting tracks in the snow.

"Whiskey my arse." Beans grabbed the stein and the bourbon. "That ol' boy's mad as a hatter."

* * * * *

Quantrill showed no ill effects of his foray with bourbon the next morning. Alistair hadn't even heard Quantrill return to the room, but woke up as the colonel washed his face in the basin, scrubbing himself furiously dry with a towel.

"Good morning, lads," Quantrill greeted.

Alistair crawled from underneath the quilt. Beside him, a groaning Beans pulled a pillow over his head.

"Captain ... er, Colonel," Alistair began while pulling on his pants.

"The bellman will send a boy up after we take our breakfast," Quantrill interrupted. "I have arranged transportation via railroad to Atlanta, and, from thence, on to Memphis. After that, we shall have to finish our route piecemeal, as we did on our journey here, via carriage, horse, and, as Beans aptly put it, 'the ankle express.'" He opened a grip, and began packing it with clothes from the chest of drawers.

"What about approaching Secretary Seddon about those girls imprisoned?" Alistair knew he was risking another verbal assault, but, criminy, he had truly believed they had traveled more than a thousand miles to Richmond specifically to get those girls out of that dungeon.

"'Those girls,' Mister Durant ... or do you mean your sister and your concubine?" Quantrill's tone was one of bemusement. He kept filling his grip while Alistair's face crimsoned.

"Lucy's not anyone's concubine!" He balled his fists.

Quantrill fastened the grip, tossed it onto his bed, and snapped: "Mister Kimbrough, if you do not get out of that bed this instant, I shall have you flogged." Then, smoothing his mustache, he walked toward Alistair. "Do you truly think a letter from that lame old war horse, Seddon, would accomplish anything, Alistair? Honestly? Do you?" His hand touched Alistair's tensed shoulder, and squeezed gently. Alistair's fists unclenched, and he felt himself slump.

"You mean well," Quantrill continued. "You have a kind heart, perhaps too kind in these dark days. President Davis signed into law an act that legitimizes our forces, irregular as we are. Yet the Yankees ignore that, and they have taken their war to our fairer sex."

Alistair stared at his stocking feet. "We haven't treated Yankee prisoners with much civility, either, sir."

With a pat on Alistair's shoulder, Quantrill moved back to finish his luggage. "Very well, Alistair," he said after a moment. "I admire a man who stands his ground, who must do something, and you have done more than your share in battle. Write your letter. I will personally deliver it to the War Department on our way to the depot. No, write two letters. One I shall deliver to Secretary Seddon and the other to President Davis. But, afterward, we must depart, and we haven't the time to wait to hear their reply."

Part of that excited Alistair. He would have preferred to learn how President Davis or Secretary Seddon would respond, but, no, maybe this would be better. A letter from him, not Quantrill, not Beans. Seddon and Davis were civilized men. They would see the injustice of imprisoning young women. They might get those girls released.

He finished dressing, found writing paper in a drawer, and sat down at the table to draft a letter, first to Secretary Seddon.

By that time, Beans Kimbrough had risen, dressed, and washed his face. Neither he nor Alistair had much to pack. Alistair figured he could roll all of his in his bedroll, even with the expensive wardrobe Quantrill had bought him.

"You hear any news from Missouri, Colonel?" Beans asked.

Quantrill tossed his last bag on the bed. "No. The fools here think the war … nay, the world … begins and ends in northern Virginia. But we must get back. I don't trust giving George Todd too much rein."

"Do you think the War Department will let you raise a regiment?"

Laughing, Quantrill shook his head. "You were in that room with Alistair and me, were you not, Mister Kimbrough?"

"So this trip was a failure?"

"Far from it." Quantrill moved from the beds to the desk, where Alistair scribbled on the paper, pausing long enough to collect his thoughts. "There are two *d*s in Seddon," Quantrill corrected, pointing. "And secretary is *r-e*, not *e-r*."

"Yes, sir." Alistair scratched through the mistakes, but Quantrill removed the pen from his hand.

"No. You start over. This must have a professional touch. You have nice handwriting, young man, easy to read, when you don't rush."

Grumbling, Alistair found new paper.

"Think before you write, young man. Choose your words carefully. It is just like aiming your revolver in battle. Make it count."

"Yes, sir."

After patting Alistair's shoulder, Quantrill turned away from the desk. "No, Mister Kimbrough, this trip was successful. You got great clothes, as did Alistair. We have new weapons, and I have a new idea. A glorious campaign that if it does not end this war, it will at least make our Partisan Rangers remembered longer than Napoleon."

Even Alistair stopped writing, craning his neck for a better look at his commander.

"You two will play important parts in this campaign, but it will be one of great risk. You have been to Kansas before, right, Beans?"

"Yeah."

Turning: "And you, Alistair?"

He shrugged. "Well, I was with y'all in Olathe." He wished he hadn't been, though.

"That's all right." Excitedly Quantrill went to help Beans finish packing. "You are educated. You are young, but experienced. No, they sha'n't question young men. Older men would be off to war. Yes, yes. I see it clearly. You now have proper attire that befits gentlemen, say, cattle buyers. You will assume new names, new identities. You both can talk like educated men, not Missouri ruffians."

"You mean …?" Beans shoved his hands into his pockets. "You're talkin' about usin' us as spies?"

"Precisely."

"Where?" Alistair asked.

That faraway gleam began brightening in Quantrill's eyes. "Torch with torch, pillage with pillage, slaughter with slaughter, subjugation with extermination," he whispered, raising his voice. "I will lay Kansas to waste." Here, he slapped Beans joyfully on the arm, and turned back to Alistair. "Finish those letters, Alistair. We waste time standing idly here."

He donned his kepi, and walked to the window. "To kill a rattlesnake, you must cut off its head. The same is true with redlegs and Abolitionists. I will lay Kansas to waste." Again his voice fell into an almost lifeless whisper. "That, Mister Secretary, is how you win a war."

LAWRENCE

CHAPTER THIRTEEN

Keeping dust off one's clothes, or even out of one's mouth, proved impossible. It was only April, but the weather had turned hot, and the wind unbearable, blowing so hard Alistair had to reach up and hold his hat on his head inside the stagecoach.

"Is it always this windy?" he managed to ask.

"*Har!*" The drummer sitting across from him laughed. "Sonny, you have yet to see a Kansas zephyr."

The coach lurched up, down, the hoofs of the mules clopping rhythmically. Beside him, Beans Kimbrough snored, his head resting on Alistair's shoulder. He wanted to move, and often fought the urge to jostle Beans awake, because they had jammed so many bodies inside the coach—and several more rode up top. Alistair could barely breathe.

"You and your partner are from …?" was pleasantly asked by the man beside the drummer, wearing a straw hat and linen duster—an experienced wayfarer, Alistair could tell.

"We are cattle buyers from the Dover Yards. Dover, Ohio." Alistair had to fish a handkerchief from his vest pocket, and wipe the grime off his lips and cheeks.

"You did not find any satisfactory beef in Saint Louis. That is where we picked you up, isn't it?"

Alistair smiled. "Yes, sir. Oh, we found beef in Saint Louis. Purchased quite a number. But my owner, Mister O'Rourke, thinks he can command a better price, make a better margin, on selling Free-State cattle to butcher shops and restaurants." He widened his grin.

"*Har!*" The drummer laughed again. "Sounds like your employer is a war profiteer."

Alistair's smile vanished. "He's my uncle, sir. With two sons serving in the Fifty-First Infantry, and another buried at Perryville, Kentucky."

"Mister White," a bespectacled lady sitting by the window next to Beans scolded. "Really."

The drummer, Mr. White, looked properly chagrined. "My apologies, lad. I meant no disrespect. 'Twas a poor attempt at humor on my part."

"Uncle Patrick is a good man, sir. An Abolitionist of the highest order. That is why he has sent my partner"—he tilted his head slightly toward Beans, who now drooled onto his coat—"and me to Lawrence."

He thought he had erred, calling that fictitious cattle buyer "Mister O'Rourke" moments earlier and "Uncle Patrick" just now, but if he had made a mistake, it appeared to have slipped past those awake in the crowded coach.

"Why aren't you and your partner in the Fifty-First Infantry?" the man in the straw hat asked.

"Mister Shea!" the woman scolded. "Of all the nerve." She was becoming Alistair's defender.

"John"—Alistair indicated again the slumbering Beans, and let bitterness creep into his voice—"and I were invalided out after Perryville. Would you like to see my scar, sir?" He reached for his side.

"That won't be necessary," the woman said.

He had a scar, too, an ugly one from the Minié ball. It looked a lot worse than it had been.

"And why aren't you fighting for the Union?" Alistair asked.

"*Har!*" The drummer had the most annoying damnyankee laugh. "Shea here is. Isn't that right, Conor?"

Conor Shea tilted his head slightly, his eyes never leaving Alistair's.

"As far as myself, young man, I saw my share of fighting before the fire-breathers ever took aim at Fort Sumter in Charleston harbor. Border ruffians, slave stealers, Missouri scum. I knew and admired John Brown, helped him free Missouri chattel at Stokesbury in '58. I—"

"Yes." The lady, Alistair's defender, cut off the Kansan. "You need not bore our young visitor." She smiled pleasantly at him. "What is Dover like, Mister …?"

"Jim Alistair," he said. "My sleeping partner is John Benedict. Dover isn't much, I guess. It's on the Ohio Canal, though, so we have blast furnaces for steel, railroads, farms, salt mines, taverns, inns. And schools, of course. My father was a schoolteacher. I don't know, ma'am. It's home, I guess." He looked at the window. "And I fear I am far from it."

At least, that part was true. In Kansas, the land of redlegs and jayhawkers, he felt far, far from Clay County, Missouri.

Leaning back, he smiled at the woman, hoping desperately that Beans would wake up, and relieve him from this interrogation. Yet he found it easy to lie. Criminy, he had never seen Ohio, let alone Dover.

"It's on the Ohio River then?" Conor Shea asked.

"No, sir. The Tuscararwas."

Quantrill had spent months drilling Beans and Alistair on Dover, on how to lie, and how to fake what might be the truth.

"That's right," Shea said. "Now I remember. It has been such a while since I've been to Dover."

It was hot, so Alistair had reason to mop his brow with the handkerchief. One reason Quantrill had told them to play the part of cattle buyers from Dover, Ohio, was that he doubted that in Lawrence, Kansas they'd run into anyone who had ever heard of Dover, Ohio.

"A lot of Irish there," Shea said. "It's grand to be Irish."

"It's grand to be Irish, sir, but Dover is mostly German. Although a number of Irish have settled there since the mills opened."

"And just a hop and a jump from Cincinnati. Now there's a great town!"

If he had said that before the comments about the river and the Irish, Shea might have been able to trip up Alistair. By then, however, Alistair was on to this man. He knew one thing about Cincinnati—coming from his travels to and from Richmond—and, honestly, not a whole lot about Dover.

"Cincinnati's spitting distance to Kentucky, sir." He turned away and managed a sheepish look at the woman. "My apologies for my language, ma'am." Again, he met Shea's eyes. "Dover's closer to Pennsylvania and Virginia than it is to Cincinnati, sir."

Shea bowed. "Geography was never my best subject in school, young man."

The mules slowed to a crawl, the driver began speaking as the stage crept carefully along. The coach rocked gently. Craning his neck, Alistair peered out the window. The dust had stopped, but not the wind, and he could see the river, knew they were on a ferry.

"Your hair," Conor Shea said, "is as long as a guerrilla's."

Alistair kept looking out the window. Down the opposite bank, a side-wheeler was pulling out of the levee, twin smokestacks belching black smoke, and a smaller packet was making its way to the landing.

"After we were invalided out of the Army," he said, not looking at Shea, "John and I decided not to cut our hair until victory is won." Part of that was true. He leaned forward even more, causing Beans to jerk awake, groggily muttering something, and wiping sleep from his eyes.

"Commendable." Shea's voice was tight.

"This is the Kaw River," Mr. White said. "South is the Wakarusa. You can cross there at Blanton's Bridge ... used to be only a crossing ... but here we use the ferry."

"Not for long," the lady said. "For soon an iron bridge will span this river."

"More progress for a great city in a great state," said a man in a bowler hat who had just awakened.

Alistair watched the slow-flowing river, felt the ferry rocking. Minutes later, they had crossed the Kaw, and the stagecoach again picked up speed. "Welcome to the Free State City, gentlemen," the drummer said. "Welcome to Lawrence."

"You appear to know much of this city, sir," Alistair said.

"Balderdash." He elbowed Mr. Shea. "Conor's your man. He came with the New England Emigrant Aid Company back in '54. Myself, I did not arrive till September of '57."

Shea cleared his throat. "Have you arranged accommodations?"

Alistair glanced at Beans, but he hadn't fully awakened.

"No, sir," he answered. "Do you have a place you would recommend?"

"The Free State Hotel is the best, but, unless I miss my guess, it will be full up. We call it the Eldridge House. But you can likely find a good room at the Johnson House on Vermont. If need be, I shall put in a word for you with the proprietor. I have some pull in this town."

Of that, Alistair had no doubt.

He could see buildings now, church steeples, wooden façades, two-, three-, even four-story structures, plus hacks, farm wagons, buggies, and plenty of Yankees—men and women, old and young, black and white. Beyond that, toward the west and north, he spied a barren mound overlooking the city.

"That hill, sir?"

"Mount Oread," Mr. Shea answered.

"*Mount!*" the drummer scoffed.

Other passengers began to come out of their slumbers. The jehu started cursing the mules, and the coach began to slow. Eventually it stopped, the doors opened, and passengers began trying to stand on wobbly feet on *terra firma*.

Alistair stamped his feet on the boardwalk until the blood seemed to circulate while Beans caught the grips tossed down by one of the stage operators. Mr. Shea removed his duster, straightened his tie and hat, and started to move on, but stopped, pointing behind him.

"This is the Johnson House," he said. "You will do me the honor of dining with my family and me at the Eldridge this evening at six o'clock? We must properly welcome you to Lawrence."

"The honor would be ours, sir." Beans Kimbrough, now fully awake, dropped the grips by Alistair's feet, bowed, and held out his hand. "I am John Benedict."

"Conor Shea. Captain, Seventh Kansas Volunteers."

After shaking, Beans said: "No uniform, Captain?"

Captain Shea did not answer, unless you counted the twinkle in his eye. "The Eldridge is on Massachusetts. You can't miss it."

"Conor!" The voice boomed in the doorway of the Johnson House, and all eyes landed on the tall man with unkempt hair that had seen neither comb nor brush, by best guess, in decades. He was gaunt, his eyes sunk deeply beneath his high forehead. "Welcome back, my good man." The words came out in wheezes, as if this wild man in good clothes was always short of breath.

"Senator." They shook hands, and quickly Shea turned, gesturing toward Alistair and Beans. "Allow me to introduce you to two young cattle buyers from Dover, Delaware."

"Delaware?" The tall man straightened to his full height. "You are far from home."

"Actually," Alistair said, "it's Ohio."

"Still. Well, welcome to the freest city in the freest state in the country. I am James Henry Lane." He held out a raw-boned hand.

Alistair took the grip Beans handed him, and felt his face pale. This was far too early, far too soon, for this to be happening. He watched nervously, wondering how he could reach his pocket pistol inside the grip, buried under shirts and ties and Dickens, before Beans Kimbrough ruined everything—and likely got them both killed here, the first day of their mission.

Beans had already recognized Lane from the Osceola raid, yet, to Alistair's surprise, Beans accepted the senator's hand, and shook it warmly. "It is an honor, sir. We have heard much about your exploits in Ohio."

"Excellent." Lane liked the praise. He moved to Alistair, who shifted his grip, and likewise shook the butcher's hand.

"Well, enjoy your stay, sirs. Conor, we must talk."

Conor Shea nodded, and turned to Alistair and Beans as the senator strode down the boardwalk. "This evening. Six o'clock," he reminded.

Speechless, the two could only nod. They stood alone moments later, the stage having pulled off, and the streets beginning to empty.

"What do we do?" Alistair glanced at his watch. It was a long time till supper.

"Walk around," Beans said. "Get the lay of things. But first, we check in." He spit in the dirt. "I must wash this hand."

* * * * *

Clean, outfitted in casual duds, and braced by excellent rye at the hotel bar, Alistair and Beans stepped back into the streets of Lawrence and began walking around.

"Five dollars a week for a hotel," Alistair complained when they were out of earshot. "That's highway robbery."

"We paid more in Richmond," Beans reminded him in a whisper.

"Yeah, but that was in Confederate script. This is Yankee money."

They found the four-story Eldridge, which looked as impressive as their hotel, and moved down Massachusetts, nodding politely and offering friendly greetings to passers-by. A black man tipped his hat at Alistair, which caused him to stutter and stare.

"'Afternoon," Beans said friendly. "Could you direct us to ... um ... Blanton's Bridge?"

"Two blocks up," the black man said, "take a right. You'll come to the ford two or so miles south of town. A stretch of the legs on a hot day like this one."

"Thank you, sir. Thank you kindly."

The Negro tipped his hat, and walked down Massachusetts.

"You act like you never seen a darky, Alistair," Beans whispered.

"Well, I haven't … I mean … one that'll look you square in the eye."

Beans was watching the black man, waiting to see if he turned back, maybe suspecting these two young spies, but the man disappeared into a haberdashery.

"Freedman," Bean guessed. "I warrant he was born in Massachusetts. Not a slave swiped from Missouri. Let's go."

They wandered about the streets, taking no notes—Quantrill had warned them about doing that—and finally headed south. Most of the streets were named after states. Yankee states. A block off Massachusetts, businesses and residences thinned. Two blocks, and they saw only the occasional house or homestead. Another block, and even fewer homes and farms.

Beans strode ahead yet another block, then stopped, turned.

"What's that hill called?"

"Mount Oread."

"I see a rider up there."

"Well, it's where I'd put a lookout," Alistair said. Since leaving Missouri, he had rarely seen any trees except along the riverbanks. From a perch up there, a body could see forever. "Speaking of which, I haven't seen any soldiers."

"We'll find them. Let's head to the river."

"The Wakarusa?" Alistair had no intention of walking a couple of miles.

"No, silly. The Kaw."

They walked east, passing one farm, then another smaller house. Closer to the river, more houses had been built, and Alistair spotted a few trees lining the western banks of the river, but much thicker woods on the higher, eastern slopes.

The street dead-ended at the Kaw, on a bluff maybe twenty feet high. Farther down, they saw a clearing and landing, but the levee for the steamboats was farther north, just below the ferry.

There were no ships on the river and not many people around, until they passed some teens hanging out on an empty lot, arguing, while one boy held the reins to two horses. The horses, Alistair noted, were strong stock. The black mare looked like a thoroughbred. They drew closer. The two horses, and, off to the right, a hobbled mule, grazing. But six or seven boys. No, one was a girl.

That's when the girl, dirty blonde hair as wild as the black's mane, jerked a pocket knife from a red-headed boy's hand. "I'll show you, Alun Cardiff!" she snapped. Quickly she opened the blade, jabbed the point between her legs, and began ripping the skirt.

"Lord have mercy!" one of the boys shouted.

"Keep walking." Beans shoved Alistair forward.

As they passed, the girl was ripping the back of her skirt. Then she dropped the knife at the redhead's feet, whirled, and grabbed the reins to the black.

That's when Alistair stopped, clenching his fists. "Looks like a horse race."

This time, Beans didn't shove him forward. He turned to watch the race.

"That's," Alistair seethed, "my mare."

Beans studied the black, saw the redhead mounting the bay.

"Dare me, will you, Alun Cardiff?" the girl said. She was already in the saddle, already kicking the black's ribs. Her hat sailed from her head. The bay wheeled, and charged after the girl on the black. The Kansas boys cheered. A few cursed.

"Nice-looking," Beans said. Long-necked, sloping shoulders, short-backed, legs hard with muscle. Yeah, she was nice-looking, a great racer, too good to be on a Clay County farm, and really too good of a horse to be in a Free-State hell hole like Lawrence. Being ridden by a girl. "I was training her," Alistair said.

"I was talking about the girl," Beans said.

The black had the lead, but the bay was strong, sleek, fast, and the red-headed boy a better, smarter rider and racer. They rode up two blocks, turned toward the river, cut back along the bluff over the levee, began thundering back.

Alistair sucked in a deep breath. The horses leaped a gully that drained into the river. The black pulled away. Maybe that girl was a better rider than the redhead.

Beside him, Beans whistled, then muttered an oath.

Alistair made himself breathe. The bay caught up, now running side-by-side with the black. Behind him, the other boys screamed, hooted, cursed.

"Hell," Beans said, "they're riding way too close …"

He hadn't finished when the bay stumbled, knocking the black to the side. The blonde girl pulled hard on the reins, but, that near the bluff, the soil was loose, soft, giving away, and the horse was screaming, going over the side. The blonde kicked free of the stirrups. Then, she was screaming, too.

Both disappeared.

Alistair found himself running, shedding his hat, his waistcoat. Behind him came a cacophony of cries, curses.

The boy on the bay reined in, swung out of the saddle, and was dashing toward the side to peer over the edge, all the while whispering: "Dear God."

Alistair leaped over the bluff. Saw the splashes made by horse and rider below. Saw the black water rushing up to meet him. Above him, just before he hit, he heard Beans' voice: "Alistair, you damned fool! You can't swim!"

CHAPTER FOURTEEN

This was not the Johnson House.

He awoke underneath a colorful quilt and atop a downy mattress, perhaps the most comfortable bed he had slept in since … Osceola? … Beans' home? Above him, white linens hung from the half canopy, while the wallpaper on the walls reminded him of all those pictures of English country gardens that he had seen in magazines. Sunlight crept through the bay window; the lavender curtains, so long they puddled on the floor, had been pulled back. Fact was, Alistair felt like he was inside some story book, until he caught the smell.

Sniffing, he quickly determined the source of the odor. "Criminy, I smell like dirty river water."

Turning his head, which hurt like the dickens, he spied a slender, young black woman walking through the open doorway. She carried a tray, which contents did not smell like dirty bath water or river water or anything bad. He was back in that story book.

"Are you hungry?" She didn't sound like any Negress he'd ever heard.

"I could eat." That had always been the common reply around his home.

She smiled, set the tray on the night stand, and helped him slide up into the bed, adjusting pillows, pulling down the quilt—he was relieved to see that he was in a nightshirt and not buck naked, until realizing that someone had undressed him to slip on this nightshirt.

"Ma'am …?" he began.

That's when things began creeping through his memories. There was a horse race. A girl. A horse stumbling, falling over the ledge. And he, not thinking, had dived in after …

"The black," he said.

"Beg your pardon, sir?"

He met the eyes of the slave—no, not a slave, but a freedwoman. After all, this was Kansas. Wasn't it?

"Where am I?" This story book had turned into a horrific nightmare. "What am I doing here? Where's Beans? What happened?"

She pressed a huge hand on his shoulder, gently eased him back against those comfortable pillows. "You rest, sir. You eat. I'll fetch Miz Iris. You're at the Shea home. You're going to be fine, yes sir, just fine. Doctor Ashley said there is nothing to worry about, that tough as you must be, nothing could kill you. Not even border ruffians."

That stopped his breath short. His hands suddenly felt clammy, and he knew he must be sweating like a race horse after eight furlongs. Suddenly he began breathing rapidly, unable to control it, and the black woman's eyes revealed fear, concern.

"Miz Iris!" she yelled. "Miz Iris!"

She left the tray on the night table, yelling over her shoulder, "I'll be right back!" hurrying through the door.

He heard her footfalls on the staircase, heard voices below. He wondered if his legs would work, would carry him out of here? Even more importantly, where had he left his Navy Colts? Footfalls and chatter came up the stairs, and then the chatter ceased, and he couldn't even hear the steps.

"*Get … a-hold … of … yourself!*" He steeled his nerves, managed to get his breathing under control, ran his fingers through his damp hair, which hurt his entire chest, and then a white woman stood in the doorway. Slight, wearing a lavish dress, dark hair flecked with gray tucked up in a bun.

"Are you all right, Mister Alistair?" she asked tentatively.

"Yes, ma'am. Just had …" He blushed. "I guess a bit of a fit." He attempted a laugh. "Nerves."

She smiled radiantly. "Are you sure, young man?"

"Yes, ma'am." He failed to match her smile. "Just waking up here. Strange home. I mean, not strange. Well, it's a fine place."

She hovered over him now, still smiling. "Welcome to the Shea house. My name is Iris Shea."

His breathing came regular now, and he wiped his hands on the sheet beneath the quilt. Shea? Yes, that's what the black servant had said.

"Let us put some food into your stomach," Iris Shea said. "You must eat to regain your strength." She did not wait for him to reply, but busied herself easing the tray onto his lap, withdrawing a silver cover that revealed a large bowl of soup. A china cup held steaming tea, and he smelled freshly baked sourdough bread.

"Shea." He tested the name. Another memory came to him savagely. "Captain Conor Shea of the Seventh Kansas."

"My husband."

"I was to dine with him."

"You were in no condition to dine with anyone last night."

"Last night?"

Iris Shea had a wonderful smile that almost relaxed Alistair. "Do you remember anything?" she asked, her smile quickly replaced by concern. "Your name, for instance?"

"It's Alistair." He caught himself before he made a fatal mistake. "Jim Alistair. Of Dover, Ohio."

"Do you remember what happened?"

"I remember jumping off a ledge like a damned …" He stopped himself, began to blush, and mumbled: "My apologies, ma'am."

Iris Shea laughed. "Young man, I have heard much worse in this household, I assure you."

"Mother!" The voice coming from outside the room was fresh, young. Footsteps sounded, then that blonde-headed rider—that brash girl who had split her skirt so she could ride like a man—entered the room. She didn't look so high-spirited now, but she was lovely, her eyes wide when she saw Alistair had not died, was sitting up in bed.

"Maura can explain," Mrs. Shea said, "and apologize. I must go to the carriage house and let the captain know that you are awake. And your friend, Mister Benedict."

The soup smelled better than it tasted. Maura Shea seemed pleasant enough, but she was no Lucy Cobb. Even Alistair's sister wouldn't have dared slit her skirts like that to mount a horse. Lucy damned well wouldn't have even considered it. Back at New Hope, the preacher would likely have excommunicated any woman so brazen.

That was a fancy dress Maura wore now. By grab, she probably had a dress for every day of the week, when, back home, a girl like Lucy Cobb or Cally Durant would have one everyday dress. When winter came, they'd rip that dress apart at the seams, then sew it back together with the inside out, to make it look new. And the Cobbs and Durants weren't even poor by Clay County standards.

When he was done eating, Maura Shea took the tray off his lap. "Would you like anything else, Mister Alistair?"

"No." After a moment, he remembered to add: "Ma'am."

"I do not blame you for being angry at me," she said.

He looked at her, suddenly realizing he'd been acting rude. But angry? Well, maybe he was. After all, he was Missourian, and this was Kansas.

The girl said: "I put you in harm's way."

"Well …" He shrugged. "I didn't have to dive into that river."

She leaned forward, placing her delicate left hand on his arm, which tingled him all over. "But you did," she said urgently. "You dived thirty feet over the bluff, into the Kaw, and you can't swim a lick!"

She removed her hand, and he looked at the arm hairs where she'd rested her fingers. He stared at that place the longest time, before making himself look up into her large, wonderful eyes.

"How'd you know I can't swim?"

"Your associate, Mister Benedict, told us."

His head bobbed slightly. "I saved your life?" he asked.

"Jim Alistair, you should be thanking those stevedores on the banks for saving both your lives," Beans announced, stepping through the threshold, his coat over his shoulder, hat in his hand. He smiled. "I'm glad to see you back amongst the living, pardner." He moved easily across the rug, dropping coat and hat on a chair, bowing gentlemanly at Maura, and sitting on the bed by Alistair's knees.

"Does he remember anything?" Beans asked Maura.

"I don't think he remembers much," she said, and looked at Alistair, eyes smiling.

"It's like this, Jim," Beans said. "The other rider knocked her horse. Accidentally, of course. Miss Maura tried to recover, and almost did, but she and her horse were too close to the bluff. So they went over. She and the horse fell thirty feet to the water below. That's when you took off at a gallop ... just leaped over the edge, boots and all."

"It was a gallant thing to do," Maura said.

"It was a fool stunt," Beans countered.

Alistair saw Conor Shea, Maura's father, standing in the doorway, fiddling with a pipe. The redleg captain said nothing.

"You hit the water. Luckily you landed in a deep pocket, else you'd all be at the undertaker's right now. I didn't dive in after you. Nor did that other rider ... what's his name?"

"Alun Cardiff," Maura answered.

"Yeah. Alun he yells for help, then takes off running south, down where the bluff ends. Some of Miss Maura's friends ran with him. Others followed me. We were heading for the landing, but, when we reached that ravine, we just climbed down in it, and it led us down to the bank. What bank there was. Not much of a chance we could get to you from there, though. I was thinking you're both dead, anyway, but some darkies were coming from the landing. They're rowing a boat like you've never seen one rowed before. I mean to tell you, that boat was flying. Well, they fished you both out of the water. I could hear Miss Maura coughing, but you weren't making a noise, so I figured you're done for. And wouldn't that be a horrible letter I'd have to write your uncle at the Dover Yards." He paused here, obviously reminding Alistair of where they were, and who they were supposed to be.

"Well, we went back up the ravine, ran down to the landing, and they've pulled you out of the boat by then. They haul you to the doctor. Must have pumped a gallon of water out of your body. By then you're moaning, so I'm thanking the Almighty for your deliverance. When Captain Shea hears about what has happened, he orders your removal from the sawbone's office to here. And here is where you are."

"I reckon," Alistair said, "I should pay those stevedores for rescuing me."

"Those wharfies have been paid in full," Captain Shea said from the room's entrance. He lit his pipe, tossed the match into a cuspidor. "Paid in full and then some. You owe such men nothing. They were all Missouri slaves … until I freed them."

He chilled the room, spoiled the mood. His daughter rose quickly, refusing to look him in the eye.

"Go help your mother," the captain ordered, and, head bowed, Maura obeyed obediently, stopping only when he said her name as she stepped toward the balustrade. "You owe Card Cardiff for saddle, bridle, and horse, Daughter."

"Yes, Father."

"And that shall be the last time you put on a riding display such as that disgusting one."

"Yes, Father."

"Go on."

She was gone, and, after drawing on his pipe and sending the blue smoke toward the linen canopy, Captain Shea spoke as he pulled up a chair near the bed. "Imagine that girl. Riding like a man. Then having to get fished out of the Kaw River by niggers."

Neither Alistair nor Beans said a word.

Captain Shea smoked his pipe.

After the silence stretched well past the awkward phase, Alistair shifted his pillows, and said: "What about the black mare she was riding, sir?"

Deliberately Conor Shea removed his pipe, and stared long and hard at Alistair. After another unbearable silence, he laughed, slapping his knee, and dropping the pipe in the tray on the bedside table. "I thought you were a cattle buyer, son, not a horse trader, but, by Jehovah, that is a question that I can appreciate. You did not dive into that river to save my daughter. It was the horse you cared about!" His callused hand slapped Alistair's covered leg as he pushed himself to his feet.

"That's a dandy, Mister Alistair. You're a lover of horses."

Of that particular horse, Alistair thought. *By grab, I trained that mare. And you, or someone in your dirty group of redlegs, stole her.* Then, he felt ashamed, for there was much truth in what Captain Shea had said. He *had* cared more for that mare.

"The river got the horse, Jim," Beans said solemnly.

"And a forty-dollar saddle and other fine tack," Captain Shea said. "Card Cardiff will likely send me a bill for killing his horse, and losing his gear."

"Cardiff, sir?"

"Alun's father. Rides with Jennison sometimes, me other times, himself sometimes." He gestured toward Beans. "You met Alun, yesterday. Isn't that right, John?"

"Yes, sir," Beans said. "Alun was the one racing …"

"I know." Alistair had heard enough. The black mare was dead, probably feeding catfish by now somewhere on the river's bottom, but that girl, Maura, was all right. And so was he. Thanks to those wharf rats by the landing.

"Well, you shall stay here," said Shea. From the tone of his voice, Alistair knew there was no room to debate and that "captain" was not an honorary rank. "Till you're on your feet."

Still, Alistair knew he could not, should not, accept. "Thank you, kindly, sir, but …"

"But nothing. That's the way it will be. I will send my manservant to the Johnson House to fetch your belongings. Mister Benedict, you are welcome here, too."

"Captain Shea, your generosity knows no bounds, but I cannot accept." Beans turned to Alistair, smiling. "It's better this way. We're here on business, and I can conduct much business in the lobby of the hotel. But you stay here, old chum. Just for a few days." His eyes narrowed, and Alistair gave a slight nod. He knew what Beans meant. Stay here. Learn about the town, about Captain Shea. About those redlegs he commanded. "I will telegraph your uncle of everything that has happened."

"No telegraph, I am afraid," Captain Shea said. "Lawrence is not as progressive as you might think."

Beans nodded. "Well, I'll write an old-fashioned letter."

"You'll want to catch up with your friend, Mister Benedict," said the captain, "but don't keep him up too long. He needs rest. I will see you downstairs in forty minutes for supper." Shea fetched his pipe and strode down the room. "It's settled," he said.

When his footsteps had faded, Beans rose. "Nothing is settled," he whispered hoarsely. "Yet."

CHAPTER FIFTEEN

The recruitment camp stood on a vacant lot along the west side of New Hampshire Street. Green kids mostly, living in canvas tents—those who owned tents, anyway—trying to learn how to drill like regular soldiers. Not many soldiers, though, and most of the men in Lawrence called those stationed here "babes." Indeed, few looked older than Alistair. A block up and over on Massachusetts Street, Negro soldiers in blue uniforms camped and drilled. Black Yankees. Honest Abe had promised these boys freedom, and they'd decided that was something worth fighting for. These were the Second Kansas Colored Regiment, under the command of the Reverend Captain Samuel Snyder, a white man. Beans figured they were all brag, though, and when the first shots were fired, those darkies and their Abolitionist captain would turn tail and skedaddle.

For as much talk as Quantrill's men had heard about Lawrence—headquarters for Jim Lane, the Free State City, the worst city in Kansas—it turned out to be not much of a town. Oh, it had plenty of people, a tad shy of three thousand, but Lawrence was really small. Downtown stretched no more than a few blocks. Some hardware stores, a gun shop run by a man named Palmer, saloons, farm stores, and a fancy, two-story mercantile known as R & B's, which carried everything and then some, including figs in air-tights, even cove oysters. A furniture store, an icehouse, a bank, not to mention an ice-cream shop and a photographic studio. The most annoying spot was Storm's Farm Machinery since every time Beans or Alistair happened by there, someone was singing or playing "John Brown's Body." Yankee flags hung in every window.

Outside the business district, houses, from three-story mansions to prairie soddies, were scattered along the open prairie and rolling hills. A deep ravine began just beyond the northwestern slope of Mount Oread and cut through the city, dividing Lawrence into east and smaller west sections, running all the way to the river.

Behind Jim Lane's home on a short avenue just off Eighth Street, a massive cornfield looked like it would produce a fine crop come harvest time, barring hail or hell. That was in West Lawrence. Also in West Lawrence was the mayor's house, just past Sixth Street, closer to the river and another ravine. The key, however, would be East Lawrence.

They'd have to take care of those soldiers. Just a few buildings down Massachusetts Street, past Seventh Street, stood the armory. They'd need to take that, too. Quickly. And capture the Eldridge House. That was the hotbed of Abolitionists, redlegs, jayhawkers, politicians, travelers, anyone who wanted to be somebody in Kansas. That's where Beans Kimbrough spent most of his evenings, laughing at Conor Shea's jokes, sharing brandy and cigars with Jim Lane, former Governor Charles Robinson, Provost Marshal Alexander Banks, Card Cardiff, and many other residents and travelers. Sometimes Beans would go to the edge of town, past the old California Road, and drink at Dulinsky's Tavern. Mentally taking names and notes.

Alastair kept a list of names hidden in the Bible he left on his bedside table. On the top were the words WHO WE WANT.

Right below that, one name topped the list, in capital letters and twice underlined:

JIM LANE, West Lawrence, near cornfield. And immediately below that: Capt. C. Shea, middle road off Tenth, foot of Mt. Oread.

The Sheas lived in East Lawrence.

* * * * *

Summer, hot and ugly, had sent spring into the deepest recesses of memories. Alistair had moved back in the Johnson House, but he still saw much of Maura Shea, practically every day. He stood in front of the mirror in his room, combing back his hair, watching the reflection of Beans Kimbrough, who laid on his bed, back propped up against the pillows and headboard, legs crossed, smoking a pipe, grinning that miserable smirk of his.

"Where's she takin' you this time, pard?" Beans asked.

"A corral." He tossed the comb on the dresser.

"What on earth for?"

Alistair grabbed his hat. "We're supposed to be buying cattle."

Beans drew deeply on the stem, holding in the smoke for a moment, then slowly exhaling. Finally he laid the pipe on the table, swung his long legs off the bed, and rose. "You're bright for a Clay County cuss, Alistair. I'll come with you."

He couldn't hide the frown, which caused Beans to slap his thighs. "You don't want me to come?"

"Come along. I don't care."

"The hell you don't." The smile vanished. Beans stepped closer. "Her pa was at Osceola. Her pa stole your mare, or one of his raiders did, anyhow. She and her entire family's Kansas dirt. Scum of the earth. Best you remember that. Best you recollect Lucy and Cally sweatin' in that hell hole back in Kansas City."

"I don't aim to forget that." He stormed out of the room, slamming the door in Beans' face.

Downstairs, he wanted to swing inside the saloon, get a bracer of rye, but Maura stood waiting in the lobby, dressed in pink calico, beaming with a lustrous smile. She rose off the sofa, and he faked a smile, taking her hands and pulling her into a brotherly embrace.

"Are you …?" She stopped, and Alistair knew why.

"Mind if I tag along with y'all?" Beans asked as he bounded down the stairs.

"Not at all." A lie. Not even a good one.

Beans started to grin, but it died as quickly as the question Maura Shea had been about to ask. He stared over their shoulders, and, slowly, Alistair turned.

"The more the merrier," Maura tried.

Alun Cardiff stood just beyond the doorway, on the boardwalk, smiling awkwardly. He stepped through the batwing doors. Nine in the morning, and already it was too hot to keep the regular doors closed. The doors flapped behind him, and he removed the kepi, revealing that bright, carrot-colored mane.

His blue trousers matched the trim of his kepi. The blouse was darker, with shiny brass buttons, and he wore a white shirt underneath. His black boots showed the signs of rigorous waxing, although the spurs didn't appear to have much use, and he carried a revolver on his hip, the flap fastened.

"Alun's coming with us," Maura said.

"If that meets your approval," the redhead said.

"Of course," Beans said. "Like Miss Maura says … 'more the merrier.'"

"Great." Alun relaxed instantly. "I have a buggy just outside."

* * * * *

"I didn't know you were in this man's army," Beans said. He sat in the front next to Alun, who flicked the reins. Alistair and Maura rode in the back seat. The top was up, providing some protection from the heat. "Do you serve with Miss Maura's father?"

"No," young Cardiff responded. "I'm with the Fourteenth Kansas. We're stationed here."

"Oh, so you're with that group behind New Hampshire?"

"For now." Alun nodded. "They say we'll likely be assigned to Jennison."

"Doc Jennison?" Beans nodded firmly. "Now, there's a good man."

Beside Alistair, Maura whispered something. Beans couldn't catch the words, but the bitterness was unmistakable.

"When are you likely to join Jennison's bunch?" Beans asked.

"There's no telling. Right now, they say we're supposed to guard the town."

Beans guffawed. "From what?"

"Exactly."

They turned down Ninth Street.

"Were you at Osceola?" Beans asked.

Alistair's stomach roiled.

Maura leaned forward, saying softly: "I wish you would not bring up that unChristian ..."

Beans whirled. "UnChristian town, ma'am?"

"Act," she said, leaning back, eyes blazing. "That was a horrific evening. The worst, most uncivilized act of this entire unpleasantness."

Beans' face relaxed. His eyes brightened. "Unpleasantness? Is that what you call this war?" Shaking his head, he nudged Alun's shoulder. "Ask me, Osceola was a blight on this earth. It needed to be wiped off the face of Missouri. Full of slaveholders and Secesh. Not a human being among the entire population."

"How would you know?" Maura demanded. "Living in Ohio?"

"Well, word gets around. We have newspapers in Dover, Miss Maura."

"Propaganda."

Beans made sure he was looking her right in the eye. "That's a big word."

"It means ..."

"I know what it means, ma'am. Are you saying that newspapers lie?"

"Sometimes."

"But your father was at Osceola." It was not a question.

"My father and I do not see eye to eye on many things."

Beans' expression immediately saddened, and he went back to staring at the mules pulling the team. "I reckon I know how you feel," he said, barely audible. "But you should …" His fingers tightened into balls, and he held his breath the longest time, finally blowing out a gust and laughing hollowly. "But this morning is too hot for a political debate. I get enough of that at the Eldridge. Look at those mules of yours, Alun. Reminds me of what Jim Lane once said, just the other night it was. We were talking about freeing slaves from Missouri trash, and Jim says … 'I would just as soon buy a nigger as a mule.' That's something, if you ask me, coming from an Abolitionist."

"He's no Abolitionist," Maura said. "He is a demagogue, or might I say a devil."

"Your father speaks highly of him, Miss Maura."

"My father is no better."

Again, Beans' fists clenched. "You should watch what you say of your pa, ma'am. One day, he could up and die on you."

"I thought we'd decided it was too hot to discuss politics," Alistair said, to which Alun echoed: "Amen."

They had turned onto Massachusetts, heading toward South Park, passing the camp of Negro recruits.

"There are true Abolitionists here, Alistair." Maura leaned so close, he could smell the fragrance of the shampoo in her blonde hair. "Not everyone in this town is an opportunist or scoundrel. Many men and women here came from New England, and we truly believe that the Negroes should be free. There are good men, good women, Christian men, Christian women. Kind men." She touched his arm. "Like you."

He wanted to tell her he was not kind at all, but he said nothing, just stared ahead. He could not even acknowledge Maura.

They did not speak again until they reached the corral.

* * * * *

Wind bent the tall grass, and Alistair stared into that endless expanse of prairie. He turned, looking back toward town, and found Mount Oread. From here, he could see one of what the Yankees called "the forts," but there didn't appear to be any lookout stationed there this morning. Nor had he seen anyone there yesterday.

A steer bawled, and, tugging his hat down so that the wind wouldn't carry it away, he headed to the corral.

Maura was calling his name excitedly. She rushed to him, grabbed his hand, urging him along. "Hurry, Jim," she said. "I wanted you to meet Reginald."

"Is Reginald the cow?"

She was about to pull his arm out of his socket. "No, silly." She called out toward the corral: "Reginald!" Then, to Alistair, whispered: "I don't care for much of what my father has done in this barbaric war, but there is some glory, some justice. Here."

A burly black man stepped off the lower corral post, and turned.

"Reginald," Maura said, "this is Jim Alistair, the cattle buyer I was telling you about. From Dover, Ohio."

"Mister …" The word died in Alistair's throat, and he almost dropped his extended hand.

Reginald was bigger, older, with weary eyes and a knotted brow. The last time Alistair had seen him had been in Osceola, at Beans Kimbrough's house.

"Hello, sir," the man said hoarsely.

"I'm …" Alistair wet his lips, trying to determine if Reginald had recognized him. "What kind of cattle are you selling?"

"Got these two steers."

Quickly Alistair climbed onto the top of the corral, eyes locking on a brindle steer. He wanted his back to Reginald.

"You raising beef?" he asked, then felt like an idiot. Of course the man raised cattle. Why else would he be meeting with a cattle buyer? Then Alistair felt sick, as if his bowels were about to release violently. Beans Kimbrough was approaching, talking, and Alistair slid his hand inside his vest, reaching for the hidden pocket pistol.

"So you're a cattle raiser? That's fine. Just fine, indeed. I'm John Benedict, sir, of Dover, Ohio. It's a pleasure to meet you, Reginald, isn't that your name, boy?"

"Yes, sir." The slave spoke without emotion, like a man facing his executioner.

"Where's your ranch, boy?"

"Betwixt Brooklyn and Baldwin City."

"I see. You married, Reginald?"

"Yes, sir."

"What's your woman's name?"

"Dilly."

"Dilly! Why, that's a crackerjack name. I used to know a Dilly in Dover. Knew a Reginald, too. That's something. That's something, indeed. How's those cattle looking, Jim?"

Deftly Alistair hopped off the corral. Beans' right hand was tucked deep inside the mule-ear pocket of his trousers, and Alistair knew he held his Derringer. Alun stood by the buggy, fidgeting with the harness on the team of mules. Maura beamed brightly at Alistair.

"Listen … Reginald, isn't it?" Alistair made a beeline, positioning him between the freed slave and Beans. "Those two steers look fine, just fine, but my uncle sent my partner, Mister Benedict, and me here to buy more than a couple of steers. Dover's not much of a city, but we'll need enough beef to supply restaurants and butcher shops all around the town and county. How long would it take you to get us, say, thirty head?"

Reginald said nothing. He just stared over Alistair's shoulder at Beans, looking as if he expected to be killed.

"Once we have all the cattle, we can herd them across the Kaw and on into Kansas City." Alistair was making all this up as he went, hoping he made sense, hoping no one caught him in a lie. "Freight them by rails up to Dover. The Dover yards will pay you top dollar. Whatever the market price is in Kansas City."

"That's fantastic!" Maura exclaimed. "Reginald, you could get with the other freedmen south of the Wakarusa, couldn't you? Could you find thirty steers for Jim … I mean, Mister Alistair?"

"Reckon," Reginald said flatly. "Take us six weeks, mayhap seven."

"That'll be just fine, Reginald," Beans said, stepping up, withdrawing his hand, empty, and extending it to his former slave. "You just stay on your farm between Brooklyn and Baldwin City then. Get those cattle ready. We'll offer you top dollar. You won't go anywhere, will you, boy?"

"No, sir."

"You'll just keep a mind on getting those beeves?"

"Yes, sir."

"Probably won't even see anybody, you'll be so busy, right, boy?"

"Yes, sir."

"'Course, I could pay you and Dilly a visit, see how things are coming along."

"Won't need to, Mister … Benedict. I know my place."

Maura moved closer, frowning. "Reginald, your place is where you want it. You're no longer a slave. You and Dilly are free. You understand that, don't you? You can barter a deal with Mister Alistair and Mister Benedict, but you don't have to."

"Yes'm. I understand all that."

Maura turned to Beans, almost spitting out the words. "And in case you have not noticed, Mister Benedict, Reginald is a *man*, not a boy."

Beans merely grinned.

"Best be gettin' back to Dilly and our place," Reginald said. "You wants me to leave these beeves here, or takes 'em back with me."

"Take them, Reginald," Alistair said dully. "Fatten them up. Fatter beef means fatter profits for you."

The old Negro moved, head hanging down, toward the corral. Beans sniggered, and walked back to the buggy.

Alistair felt Maura's fingers intertwine with his, and she squeezed.

"Oh, Jim," she said, "this is so wonderful."

"Yeah," he managed to say. "Wonderful."

CHAPTER SIXTEEN

"We need to light a shuck." The door to their hotel room slammed shut. "Now."

Alistair made a beeline for the armoire, finding his grip, his clothes, but Beans had casually flung off his hat, and flopped on the mattress, not even bothering to remove his brogans. "We ain't goin' nowhere, pard. Till Colonel Quantrill sends for us."

"Reginald will tell …"

"That ol' boy won't say nothing. He knows better." Beans found his pipe and tobacco pouch. "Besides, Dilly won't let him get me hanged. She loves me. Yes, sir, Reginald and Dilly are good niggers. They'll do right." He pulled on the drawstrings of the pouch. "They know I'll kill 'em if they don't."

Knees turning weak, Alistair sank into the chair. "That's a big gamble," he said weakly.

Beans tamped tobacco into the clay bowl, found a match, and struck it against the wall. "It's no gamble at all." Once he had the tobacco glowing, his tone serious, he said, losing that hayseed accent: "If I wasn't certain, I'd be packing like you want. Last thing I desire, pard, is to get you killed. Or me." Laughing, Beans picked up the newspaper he had liberated from the lobby of the hotel, and tossed it to Alistair. "Here I am spying for the Cause, and I'm still becoming more famous. Bottom right-hand corner."

The headline in the Leavenworth *Conservative* exclaimed:

BARBARIC ACT BY THAT BUTCHER BEANS!

Alistair read:

Reports reached this office late yesterday evening of a bloody ambush of Federal forces near the Village of Westport, Missouri, on the afternoon of the sixteenth instant.

The Ninth Kansas Cavalry, one hundred and fifty strong, were heading to their encampment when a band of bushwhackers charged out of the brush, screaming like the devil incarnates they are, pistols in both hands, reins in their teeth, sending heavy, deadly leaden balls with much devastating effect.

Our noble Free State contingent tried to stand their ground, but these ruffians are experienced pistol fighters and equestrians of high renown. After a gallant stand, the Federals broke ranks and retreated for Westport, while the renegades circled the remnants and cut them down.

It was afterward that the real horror began.

When troops were organized in the village and sent back to the martyred battleground, what they found would sicken the strongest stomachs. Twenty heroes lay naked on the ground. All had been scalped, and most of those brave soldiers suffered other depredations too barbaric to describe in this newspaper. One note was found pinned to the chest of a fallen Kansan.

"Killed by Beans Kimbrough," the note read. "Remember Osceola."

Kimbrough, of course, is the butcher of several soldiers

in a ghastly ambush in Clay County last autumn. His name is as reviled as the names of Quantrill, Todd, Mosby, Morgan, savage Indians to our west, and even Satan himself to our south. Or, perhaps, as we are beginning to believe, Beans Kimbrough is, indeed, Lucifer.

Slowly Alistair lowered the paper. "You weren't there."

"You should be a detective." Beans snatched the paper, glanced at the headline again, and chuckled. "Probably Arch Clements' idea of a joke. And it's a good one. Next time I see him, I'll have to buy Arch a Punch cigar."

"I still think we should hightail it for the Sni-A-Bar."

Beans tapped the pipe bowl on the table. "Our orders are to stay until we are sent for."

"Since when did you follow orders?"

This time, Beans' chuckles even caused Alistair to smile. Shaking his head in disbelief, Alistair sank back into the chair, reaching for the bottle of rye. "You're going to get us both killed, Beans," he said.

"Well, we'll die game. But not before that Independence Day celebration. I hear it'll be one fine fandango. Pass me that bottle, old chum, won't you?"

* * * * *

Lawrence turned out in its Sunday finest. Red, white, and blue bunting hung from each resplendent building along Massachusetts Street, and a brass band had gathered in front of the Eldridge. American flags waved from the hands of men, women, and children. The white-haired Methodist minister led the assembly—by Alistair's guess, the whole damned town—in prayer, the mayor gave a quick speech, Jim Lane a longer one, and then the horns began blasting "Yankee Doodle Dandy" and the crowd followed the parade.

Up the avenue, down Eighth Street for a block, then back down

New Hampshire, all the way down to the City Hotel, and then up and over and down to the ferry and the flagpole.

The Liberty Pole.

It stood at the end of Massachusetts Street, where the ferry crossed the Kaw River, and where material was piled up for the new bridge the city had planned. A giant Stars and Stripes hung limp, for, on this rarest of Kansas days, the wind did not blow. Yet. Underneath the pole stood those raw recruits of the four-teenth Kansas, twenty-some-odd boys. Standing at the head of the bluecoats, musket on his shoulder, was Alun Cardiff. Just behind the bluecoats stood, at attention, the Negro troopers and their white preacher-captain.

The band finished "The Battle Cry of Freedom," and another preacher launched into his commands to God. To end the rebellion. To end slavery. To deliver everyone from evil. To smote Quantrill, Jefferson Davis, and Beans Kimbrough.

At that, Beans nudged Alistair's arm, and chuckled.

Next came the Reverend Captain Snyder, but he spoke without anger, merely bowed his head and asked everyone to follow him in "The Lord's Prayer."

As soon as the parson put an "Amen" onto his prayer, the mood around the riverfront changed. Alun Cardiff barked an order, the Kansas recruits did their best to turn and march off to the left to their commanders. The black soldiers then stepped forward, and began singing, their voices haunting, deep, and resonate. It was some spiritual that Alistair had never heard.

When they had finished, they marched off behind the white soldiers.

Another woman began singing, a cappella.

> Just as I am, without one plea
> But that thy blood was shed for me,
> And that thou bidd'st me to come to thee,
> O, Lamb of God, I come.

To Alistair's surprise, he heard Beans singing along with her. Alistair only mouthed the words. He couldn't see through the crowd, to see who this woman was, and when she had finished, four men began bellowing "Rock of Ages."

After that, the crowd quieted, but then another voice began, and Alistair caught his breath. At first, he thought it was Lucy Cobb, but, no, this voice was softer, more polished.

> We shall meet but we shall miss him.
> There will be one vacant chair.
> We shall linger to caress him
> While we breathe our ev'ning prayer.
> When one year ago we gathered,
> Joy was in his mild blue eye.
> Now the golden cord is severed,
> And our hopes in ruin lie.

Other voices melded into one, but by then Alistair knew who was leading the crowd in "The Vacant Chair." Beside him, Beans Kimbrough did not mouth the words, but shook his head, turning his attention to those blue-coated soldiers, black and white. He caught Alistair's glance, and said: "That song seems to follow you like a stray dog.

Alistair opened his mouth, but no words came out.

The crowd had joined in.

> True, they tell us wreaths of glory
> Evermore will deck his brow,
> But this soothes the anguish only,
> Sweeping o'er our heartstrings now.
> Sleep today, O early fallen,
> In thy green and narrow bed.
> Dirges from the pine and cypress
> Mingle with the tears we shed.

"Frank's old lady was right," Beans said softly. "Yankee song."

"Be careful," Alistair warned, although no one nearby could have heard Beans' comment.

"But I reckon Miss Maura does sound a mite better than Miss Lucy. Don't you reckon?"

A silver-haired woman in blue and white dress turned, staring, smiling. Alistair remembered her face, but not her name. He had helped her carry some packages out of Fillmore's Dry Goods to her wagon. Alistair gave her a friendly nod, and began singing the chorus.

We shall meet, but we shall miss him.
There will be one vacant chair.
We shall linger to caress him
While we breathe our ev'ning prayer.

The lady's head bobbed in approval before she resumed staring into the backs of hats and parasols.

* * * * *

By the time they had returned downtown, the streets were lined with tables piled high with food. Beef, potatoes, biscuits, corn-bread, turkey, ham, fried chicken, squash, jellies, beans, corn, carrots, turnips, parsnips, pots of coffee, pitchers of lemonade, kegs of beer, jugs of wine. More pies, cakes, and cookies than Alistair had ever seen.

Blacks and whites talked and ate together. Their children played together. Ladies chatted about their recipes, farmers looked at the sky for a chance of rain, and men like Lane and Shea and others discussed politics and the war.

"Hello!"

Alistair had just bit into a buttery biscuit. Crumbs fell onto the front of his vest, and he tried to brush them off, but wound up dropping the biscuit, which a dog promptly devoured.

"I fear I have ruined your dinner," Maura Shea said.

"No, ma'am." Alistair wiped his mouth. "I don't think the ladies, or me, will miss that biscuit much."

Giggling, she walked to his side. "So how does our celebration of the Fourth of July compare to Dover, Ohio's?"

Beans had brought over two mugs of beer, handing one to Alistair. With that boyish grin, he offered the other to Maura, who smiled while shaking her head.

"Lemonade then?" Beans asked.

"If it's no bother."

"No bother at all, Miss Maura." He waded between an American flag and a freedman, and the crowd swallowed him.

"So ... Lawrence or Dover?" Maura asked again.

He had to sip his beer to think. When was the last time they'd celebrated Independence Day in Clay County? Two years back? Three? Or had they stopped during the border wars? Maybe he had merely pushed such memories in an unreachable part of his brain.

Setting the beer on the edge of the table, he smiled. "Maura," he said, "I don't think any city in our country could compare to this celebration."

Lying had become as natural to him as it came to Beans.

"You sing lovely," he said. Which was no lie.

"Have you heard that song before?"

He wasn't prepared for that question, and his face fell. She saw the hurt, and stepped closer. "Yes," he managed to choke out. She reached for his hand, but he pulled it away before she could trap him.

"It was at a funeral," he said, and then the lies came flowing again, easily, smoothly. "For our captain. He died leading a charge with the Fifty-First Infantry in Kentucky."

She found a way to grab his hand anyway. "I'm sorry, Jim." Tears welled in her eyes. "It might help to know that Henry

Washburn wrote that song ... a poem, actually ... for Lieutenant John Grout, who was killed at Bull Run. John was only eighteen years old when he fell. He came from Worcester, same as me, although I did not know him personally. And ..."

"Yes, ma'am," he said. "I know." He knew nothing about that song, other than the fact that Maura Shea sang it much better than Lucy Cobb.

He felt her squeezing his hand, and saw her bring it to her lips. He felt her kiss.

"I'm so sorry for causing unpleasant memories, Jim."

She released his hand, and it dropped by his side. His side began throbbing from where the Yankee ball had left a ragged scar. That wound hadn't bothered him in months.

"It's ..." He had no more lies left in him.

"Lemonade, Miss Maura. It's lemonade!" Beans Kimbrough thrust a glass into her hand. Beans raised his mug in toast. "Happy Independence Day!"

* * * * *

On the last night of July, a bell began tolling.

At first, Alistair thought it must be some prank. Boys pulling kid stuff, but he could hear people filing out onto the street, and, despite the pillow over his head, he could make out muffled shouts. Beans tossed off the covers and crept to the window, drawing back the curtain, peering into the moonlight street.

The bell's pealings never ceased.

"Somebody getting married?" Alistair wondered, giving up and swinging out of the bed.

"Not unless they're getting hitched at the armory." Beans checked his watch. "At midnight."

The moon bathed the streets in pale light, and Beans sniggered as he raised the window, saying: "Criminy. They're running around like ants."

As soon as the window opened, shouts carried up, immediately wiping out any weariness Beans and Alistair felt.

"Bushwhackers are coming! Bushwhackers are coming! Get your guns, boys! Get your guns!"

CHAPTER SEVENTEEN

It had been a false alarm, and those citizens of Lawrence, terrified and praying for deliverance just moments earlier, scurried back to their homes bickering, cursing, complaining. The cannon had been wheeled out in front of the Eldridge, and left there when the militia realized there was no one to fight. Soldiers, both white and black recruits, came running to the armory—those who hadn't fled in terror to the ravines and woods—half dressed, some not even carrying their muskets. Even Alun Cardiff looked terrified, until he realized that no Missourians were charging down Massachusetts, ready to sack the town as border ruffians had done back in 1856.

In the moonlight, Jim Lane and Alun's father, Card Cardiff, railed at those soldiers, cursing them as cowards. Waving a jeweled sword overhead, Lane bellowed at the sentry who had sounded the alarm. Mayor George Collamore hung his head in shame.

A long-haired man, dressed in buckskins, galloped down the street, brandishing ivory-handled pistols in both hands. "Where are they?" he yelled. "Where are the scoundrels?"

"Still in Cass County," came an acerbic reply.

The man in buckskins cursed, slid his revolvers into the saddle holsters, turned his roan, and galloped back toward Mount Oread.

"A most interesting display." Beans chuckled. "Most interesting, indeed."

"Do you really think …?" A woman began, pointing her Bible under Conor Shea's chin. Shea's hair was tangled, his nightshirt hastily tucked inside his striped britches, a Remington revolver stuck inside a mule-ear pocket. "Do you really think Missouri riff-raff would raid us? In Lawrence? Forty miles from the safety of their god-forsaken state?"

Shea said nothing. The woman turned indignantly, and hurried home.

"It would be not only impossible," a man chided the major, "but ridiculous."

Still sniggering, Beans headed back toward the Johnson House.

* * * * *

Memories of the madness of that night quickly evaporated.

The newly organized Eleventh Kansas Cavalry left Kansas City, captured the Secessionist stronghold of Nevada City in Vernon County, Missouri, and left the town in flames.

Lawrence celebrated.

Vicksburg had fallen. Robert E. Lee's Army of Northern Virginia, once seemingly invincible, had been turned back at some place in Pennsylvania called Gettysburg.

Lawrence celebrated.

Corn grew tall. Melons and tomatoes ripened.

Lawrence celebrated.

The Reverend Lowman preached one Sunday from his pulpit, not fire and brimstone and death to bushwhackers and slave owners, of fear and war and rumors of war, but rather a sermon of hope. "The beginning of the end appears unmistakably," he said. "Hope, at long last, begins to smile over our wonderful land."

Lawrence celebrated.

Every evening, concerts or lectures or dances were held underneath the Liberty Pole. There were Bible readings. Recitals. Soliloquies from Shakespeare. Prayer meetings. Strains of "Yankee Doodle" and "Johnny, I Hardly Knew Ye" rang out across the streets. Word began coming that the telegraph would soon link Lawrence with the rest of these United States. That the rails of the Pacific Railroad would arrive a short time after the telegraph.

Lawrence celebrated.

Upstairs in his room, Alistair sat alone, trying to make some rhyme or reason out of *The Shaving of Shagpat: An Arabian Entertainment*, a strange novel published in London by some writer he had never heard of. He wasn't interested in reading, especially about a Persian barber and an enchantress and some magical sword. He had his own fantasy.

If the war ended …

Which made him surprisingly happy. It didn't matter if the North won, or the South. The war would be over. Lucy and Cally would be freed. Lawrence, and Maura Shea, would be spared. He would be spared, of having to face Maura, having to see the faces of those people he had befriended in this town, having them see what a traitor, what a butcher he truly was.

If the war ended, he could go home, back to Lucy and his parents. Providing the Yankees would let those Partisan Rangers alone, not try to hang them. If the Yankees kept considering him an outlaw, not a real soldier, well, he could always continue to be Jim Alistair, cattle buyer, a good man. He could hang his hat in Lawrence—with Maura.

August brought an intense, almost unbearable, heat, and Alistair closed the book, tossed it on the table, and moved to the window, hoping to catch a breeze. Across the street, he saw Beans, chatting with a bluecoat, handing the Yank a cigar before crossing Vermont, pausing to let a freight wagon pass, and finally disappearing underneath the awning.

The breeze did not help. Alistair moved away from the window to the dresser. He poured water from the pitcher into a glass, and drank. Refilled. Drank again.

The door opened, and Beans slid in quickly. Another man followed, and Alistair instantly dropped the glass, and reached for his pocket .31. The man raised his head, removed his straw hat, and Alistair took a step back.

It was Frank James.

"Pay your bill," Frank said. "Check out. Can you get horses?"

"We'll have to rent them from the livery," Beans said.

"Do it."

"We can say we're going to go looking for cattle," Beans went on. "Check on those darkies on the far side of the Wakarusa."

"Whatever you think sounds best. Just meet me and Henry Wilson at Blanton's Bridge. *Pronto.*"

Frank gripped the knob, opened the door, checked the hallway, then slid out of the room. "Something horrible's happened back home," he said, and, as he closed the door, Alistair could just barely hear him whisper: "And the day of reckoning is coming."

MISSOURI

CHAPTER EIGHTEEN

Slowly the cortège moved through Centerville. Two mules pulled the cart that carried a lone pine coffin, the top laden with roses, wildflowers, and a wreath.

A wreath of glory? Alistair thought, then brushed aside a tear.

On the left side of the road, just beyond the small town, he sat in the saddle on a blood bay, watching the solemn rider lead the coffin out of Centerville and into the country. Alistair's heart ached, like it had been pierced by a dozen Yankee balls. Balls that could only torture, not kill.

Then came the farm wagon, driven by Mr. Todd, and, dressed in black. Beside him, wailing like a woman who had lost all reason, Mrs. Cobb cried in anguish.

Alistair dared not look at her. He made himself focus on Frank James, mounted on a dun horse on the other side of the street. Draping the reins over his horse, Frank removed his slouch hat with his left hand as the procession passed. His right hand gripped a Remington .44, in plain view.

Alistair remembered another time, an eternity ago, when they had attended another funeral. He recalled Frank's words about Mrs. Cobb: "Not strong stock like most Clay County farm mothers." *Well, how many mothers could stand losing a son in this horrific war*, Alistair thought, *... and now ... a ... daughter?*

He groaned, and could not dam the tears that washed down his cheeks but could not clean his face, his soul.

The parson from New Hope followed on foot, hatless, head bowed, clutching a Bible in both hands, muttering a silent prayer.

Other mourners followed, solemn, silent, some with Bibles, others with shotguns, muskets, revolvers. When the last passed, Frank nudged the dun, Alistair kneed the blood bay, and they joined two other riders who kept the rear guard: Beans Kimbrough, and William Quantrill.

The bay gelding wasn't the horse he had rented from the Lawrence livery. That horse wouldn't do in a fight, so Alistair had traded it and $30 for one of Jim Cummins' spare mounts. Likewise, Beans Kimbrough also rode a good thoroughbred.

Silently they followed all the way to the Cobb farm, but the riders stopped on the pike, not turning down the path toward the farmhouse, not following the mourners.

Quantrill faced the riders: "I will pay my respects, but I fear it unwise, and not desirable for Missus Cobb's health, to have us all so close as she buries dear Lucy." He addressed everyone, but his eyes burned into Alistair. "Is this amenable to you, sir?"

Alistair wet his lips, but could not speak. His head barely bobbed.

"You may pay your respects at your own home, Alistair," Quantrill said. "See your sister."

"I saw her yesterday." He could speak, after all. He wanted to add: *Would to God I had not.*

"Beans?" Quantrill asked.

"I druther picture Cally when she was whole."

Again Alistair's heart burst.

"What the hell happened?" Beans broke the silence with a cry of exasperation.

They knew. Well, they thought they knew.

On August 13, that three-story brick building the Yankees had turned into a "Female Prison" in Kansas City had collapsed.

Practically every Secesh or Southern sympathizer in Western Missouri believed that those walls had not tumbled down on their own. This wasn't Jericho. No act of God. Yankees, soulless sons-of-Satan, had murdered six girls, not a one more than twenty years old, some as young as nine. Scores more had been scarred, maimed, crippled. Their only crimes had been their names. They were kin to the boys who rode with Quantrill.

Bloody Bill Anderson's sister was dead. Another sister maimed for life. Charity Kerr, sister of John McCorkle and cousin of Cole Younger, was dead. Soon Lucy Cobb would lay six feet under beside her brother Tommy. The last words anyone had heard from her had been: "Please, God, get these bricks off my head."

Cally Durant might have escaped unharmed, but, two weeks earlier, the Yanks had fastened a fifteen-pound ball to the chain around her ankle. A doctor from Liberty said she would never walk again. Nor use her right hand, which had been crushed.

"This was murder," Quantrill said. "A most fiendish plot. But the Yankees shall pay. We meet at the Perdee place tonight. I will see you there." He wheeled his mount, and hurried around the bend.

Slowly Frank James, Beans, and Alistair turned their horses around. They rode at a walk, then a trot, and finally a canter. Never once, until they had reached Perdee's farm, did they holster their revolvers.

* * * * *

"It was murder!" Bill Anderson screamed.

He looked like a ghost, a man already dead, and his eyes revealed a madness that had consumed him. His hands gripped the knotted yellow cord, twisting, tightening, his knuckles as pale as his face.

No one in camp spoke to Anderson. They just let him rant.

"I'll see to your horses." Henry Wilson took the reins from

Beans and Alistair. Clell Miller led Frank James' horse to the picket line. "Get some coffee," Henry Wilson told them. "There's a mess of corndodgers in that sack by the fire."

They moved from the corral toward the fire, passing men, men who said nothing. Cole Younger sat on a rock, flames illuminating his face, but his eyes seemed dead, also. He looked older, too.

"It was murder!" Bill Anderson screamed.

Silently sitting by the fire, Dill McCoy filled two tin mugs with coffee, and handed them to Beans and Alistair.

"Murder!" Anderson paced back and forth. "As God is my witness, Josephine, I shall avenge you! Their holy temple we shall defile! We shall lay their Jerusalem on heaps. The dead bodies of their servants will become meat unto the fowls of the heaven, the flesh of thy saints unto the beasts of the earth! Their blood shall shed like water. And there shall be none to bury them!"

Few slept that night, and when Quantrill returned before dawn, he met briefly with Beans and Alistair. Beans handed him the "Who We Want" list, which Quantrill eyed quickly, folded, and passed to John Jarrette.

"How many men have we?" Quantrill asked.

"Two hundred and fifty," Jarrette answered.

That figure made Alistair turn. He hadn't realized so many men had arrived in camp, hadn't fathomed just how many people now sided with the Partisan Rangers.

"I thought more would join us," Quantrill said, "now." Sighing, he wolfed down a cold biscuit, and walked to the fire, Jarrette, Beans, and Alistair following.

"I ride to Lawrence," Quantrill said after climbing atop a stump. No one spoke.

"Kansans have murdered, robbed, burned, pillaged. They have stolen our property, our slaves, our dignity. Now they have robbed us of our loved ones. Our women. Our daughters. And Lawrence is the greatest hotbed of Abolitionism. We can exact revenge, and bounty, by raiding this city. We will make them regret Osceola. We will make them mourn Nevada City. My plan is to divide whatever money we reap evenly amongst ourselves."

Alistair frowned, staring at the back of Quantrill's head. He had abruptly changed from revenge to looting.

"You can divide it among the needy if such is your desire," he said. "We will leave Lawrence in ruin, and we will return rich, and our thirst for vengeance, for those martyred heroines in Kansas City, slaked."

Silence.

Alistair felt sick.

"That's a fool's play, Colonel!" someone called out in the darkness.

To Alistair's surprise, Quantrill nodded. "Yes. I consider it almost a forlorn hope. Honestly I don't know how many of us shall return. But ..."—he gripped the butts of his revolvers—"if you dare not risk, you never shall gain."

No one else said a word, and Quantrill frowned. After a long while he jutted his jaw at Bill Anderson, who had been silent for almost six hours now.

"What say you, Bloody Bill?" A boyish excitement blazed in Quantrill's eyes.

Anderson did not even look up. "It is Lawrence or hell," he said. "But with one proviso. We kill every male thing. She has sown the wind. Let her reap the whirlwind."

Quantrill turned, blue eyes now on Beans. "What say you, Kimbrough?"

"Lawrence," Beans answered hoarsely. "Remember our girls. Remember Osceola."

"Aye!" George Todd called out, "An eye for an eye."

Added Chris Kennard: "And a tooth for a tooth."

Other comments drifted through the camp as the sky began to lighten. Everyone called for Lawrence, no matter the odds. Surprisingly Frank James said nothing, and he had as much reason to lobby for a raid as anyone who had lost a loved one in Kansas City. On the ride to Centerville, Frank had told Beans and Alistair how Yanks had raided his mother's farm, whipped his brother Jesse, then stretched their stepfather's neck with a rope, almost killing the old man. Just to learn where Frank James was hiding, where Quantrill might be camped.

Equally quiet was Cole Younger, whose cousin had been killed at the prison. His vacant eyes looked at the dying embers in his campfire, not at Quantrill, not at any of the other bush-whackers, lost in his own thoughts.

"Alistair?"

His head jerked, and Quantrill's pale eyes burned through him, held him captive. He wanted to say no, that this was indeed a fool's play, that enough people had died already, that, hell's fire, the war was practically over. He heard Maura Shea singing "The Vacant Chair," and then he pictured Lucy Cobb. Dead. Crushed by brick walls. Buried alive. As if the Yankees had stoned her to death.

"Lawrence," he said.

KANSAS

CHAPTER NINETEEN

August 21, 1863

Brother Sam Snyder was the first to die.

Alistair remembered him, the old minister of some congregation known as the United Brethren Church, the kindly commander of the Second Kansas Colored Regiment.

Just last month, on that Fourth of July, standing in front of the Miller Block, Snyder had handed Alistair a piece of lemon cake.

"Isn't it great to be alive," the reverend-captain had said, "eating cake, and loving our country, loving all men regardless of the color of their skin?"

On that Friday morning, Snyder was sitting on a stool, milking his cow, when they rode to his farmhouse as dawn began to break.

"Good morning," were the last words he said.

He had raised his hand to shield his eyes, but did not stand, likely thinking they were Kansas militia.

One of the new boys took the cow with him, but they did not burn the house. When they rode off toward town, Snyder lay on his back, his sobbing widow cradling his head in bloodstained arms.

* * * * *

They had left Perdee's at daybreak on the nneteenth, riding all day until they came to the Potter farm near Lone Jack at sundown. There, they had rested their horses, taken supper, and slept for an hour or so. At 8:00 p.m., they had saddled up, and rode. A hundred men from Clay County had joined them at the middle fork of the Grand River around dawn. Another fifty arrived from Bates and Cass Counties. None had flinched when Quantrill revealed where they were bound. They'd merely tightened their cinches, and checked the percussion caps on their revolvers.

In the timber along the riverbanks, they had rested, slept, waited all the day of the twentieth, mounting again in late afternoon, riding, crossing into Kansas, by best guess, in the darkness around 6:00 p.m. They had ridden through Spring Hill, through Gardner, and Hesper, stopping only to rest their horses, and make sure no Federals followed.

Now they stood in their stirrups, southeast of Lawrence. Four hundred strong. They carried no flag. They could see Mount Oread, the white smoke of breakfast fires serpentining out of chimneys into a pale, cloudless sky. They could see the spires of church steeples. Slowly they began shedding Union blue blouses and shell jackets that covered their embroidered shirts.

Quantrill turned his horse, facing the boys. "I need not tell you why we are here!" he shouted. "This is the home of Jennison and Lane. They have given us no quarter. Nor shall we. Kill every soldier."

"Every *man!*" Bloody Bill Anderson bellowed, yet Quantrill ignored him.

"But anyone who harms a woman or child shall answer to me."

"Damnation!" George Todd eased his horse out of formation, pointing the barrel of an Army Colt. "We have been spotted!"

Knowing Lawrence better than most of the raiders, Beans and Alistair rode near the point. Alistair kicked the blood bay forward, and looked. Two riders were trotting toward them, but had stopped. The rider on a black took off at a gallop.

Alistair swore.

"Hey," Todd shouted, "one of 'em's ridin' side-saddle!"

She stayed put.

"I'll get the other bastard!" Oll Shepherd loped after the one fleeing toward the cornfield.

Alistair spurred the bay, drawing one of his Navies. "He's mine!"

Out of the corner of his eye, he saw Todd, Quantrill, and the rest racing toward the girl on the white horse. Over the pounding of hoofs, the air rushing past his ears, he could hear Shepherd's curses, and Maura Shea's screams: "Hurry, Alun! Hurry! Ride! Ride like the wind!"

She kicked the mare into a run, heading toward town, but, even as good a rider as Maura was, Alistair knew that she'd never outrun the boys. Not side-saddle. The irony would not strike him until much later. Had Conor Shea not insisted that his daughter never ride like a man again, she might have been able to warn the town.

He just prayed the boys would remember Colonel Quantrill's warning about not harming a woman.

He pulled even with Shepherd, who grunted, spit, brought the reins into his mouth, and drew another revolver with his left hand. By then, however, the bay had exploded past Shepherd. Alistair had not seen the day when Oll Shepherd, big as he was, could outride him.

The black leaped a fence. Alun was a magnificent rider. Alistair's bay did not even slow, clearing the top rail easily, landing perfectly, not missing a beat. He thumbed back the hammer, aimed, and slumped in the saddle as he jerked the trigger.

Ahead, Alun leaned lower.

He must not be carrying a weapon, Alistair thought, wondering why Alun was not in camp with the other recruits. A leave? Preferential treatment? Or maybe the Kansans had as much discipline as Quantrill's troops. Alistair fired, turned, saw Oll still riding, having also cleared the fence. He could not see Maura. Quantrill's men had surrounded her.

The black cleared a ditch. So did the bay.

Both horses plowed into the cornfield, the stalks and long leaves whipping horses and riders, then moving out into rolling prairie. Alistair had lost his hat. Alun's kepi had been knocked off.

Alistair fired again, deliberately missing. Alun swung out of the saddle, and dived into the heavily wooded ravine. The black took a few steps, and snorted. Salty froth lathered its coat. That horse wouldn't have been able to have carried Alun much farther.

Reining up, Alistair fired one round into the trees, then holstered the Navy. Oll Shepherd slid his brown mare to a stop, cursing, snapping a futile shot himself. "Why don't you go after him?"

"In those woods?" Alistair wheeled his horse. "We'd never flush him out. Besides, he can't warn anyone. Let's get back to the others."

He gave Shepherd no time to argue, and kicked the bay into a hard run, back over the ditch, through the cornfield, jumping the fence, glancing once just to make sure Oll Shepherd was riding behind him. He was. Alun Cardiff was safe.

For now.

He reined in the bay in front of Quantrill. "He got into a thicket, sir. But he's too far from town to sound the alarm." Oll Shepherd came trotting up beside him, confirming Alistair's report.

"Very well." Quantrill gestured over his shoulder. "Todd, Anderson, Jarrette, take your men and hit the soldier camps. Cut them down like the snakes they are. Kimbrough, you find Lane. Kill him. Shepherd, this woman will guide you to the homes of the other men we want. How is your horse, Durant?"

"Pretty winded, Colonel," Alistair lied.

"Then you shall accompany Shepherd."

Quantrill's horse was jittery, bouncing, fighting the bit. "McCoy, Kennard. To the top of that hill. You are our lookouts. Let us know when you see dust. The dust will mean the Yankees are on their way. The rest of you, to the Eldridge!"

The army of killers galloped toward town, Quantrill at the head of the charge. Mounds of dust forced Alistair to turn his head. He even coughed. When the powdering cleared, settled, he wiped his face, longing for a sip of water, but then saw Maura Shea, her face paled by shock, by revulsion.

"Jim?" she whispered.

"It's Alistair," he said. "Alistair Durant. Of Clay County, Missouri, ma'am." He choked down the bile rising in his throat, and barked out at Shepherd. "Come on. You heard the colonel's orders!"

*　*　*　*　*

Eighteen rode with Shepherd, Maura riding between Oll and Alistair. They stopped first at a two-story farmhouse surrounded by a good cornfield.

"Who lives here?" Shepherd asked Maura.

"I don't know," she answered stiffly.

Shepherd glanced at Alistair, who shrugged. "It's a big town, Oll. Lot of farms around here. I don't know who lives here, either."

"Somebody's beat us to it, Oll!" one of the newcomers called out. "Barn's already a-burnin'."

"Hell." Still, Shepherd nudged the brown mare forward, and they rode to the farmhouse.

Two of the boys stood in the garden, but their faces were unfamiliar. One bit into a slice of cantaloupe, the thick juice streaming down his pockmarked face. The other leaned against a scarecrow, putting a fresh cylinder into his Remington. Beside them, between a row of beans and tomatoes, lay a bald man, the back of his head blown off.

The one pitched the rind onto the corpse, wiped his mouth, and saw the newcomers. "Y'all missed the fun," he said, and he and his comrade left the dead man, trampling the plants, as they found their horses, mounted, and rode toward town.

By that time, the slamming of a screen door drew Alistair's attention. Two long-haired, bearded men, some of the newcomers from Bates County, came out of the house, already billowing smoke. One carried two silver candleholders, which he stuffed inside his saddlebag. They swung into their saddles, and followed the two others toward Lawrence.

A slender woman charged out of the house, screaming: "Help me! Help me! For the love of God, please help me." She dropped a china pitcher on the grass, and ran back inside. When she came out, she was coughing, scattering three tintypes and some silly glass figurine beside the pitcher. "Help!" Smut and grime covered her face. She tried to move back into the burning house, but her knees buckled, and she fell, pleading: "Help … me."

Alistair felt himself swinging off the bay, but, to his surprise, by the time his feet touched the ground, Oll Shepherd was already moving toward the screen door. In less than a minute, they came out, sweating, eyes burning, Oll carrying a mirror, and Alistair dragging a rocking chair. These they placed beside the sobbing woman, and went back in. When they returned, coughing raggedly, sucking in deep breaths of hot air, they lowered a pie safe—the paint on one side having bubbled from the heat of the flames—onto the ground beside the hysterical widow. Alistair wiped his face, and started for the door, but Oll grabbed his arm, and jerked him back.

"No use," he said. "Let's get out of here."

Inside, came the shattering of glass. Flames leaped out of the lower windows. Smoke poured from the door. The roaring of the blaze intensified as Alistair turned for his horse.

The woman grabbed his left hand, brought it to her mouth, kissing it repeatedly. "Thank you," she gasped. "Thank you. Thank you." She was still thanking him, between sobs, as he pulled away, grabbed the reins, and swung back into the saddle.

"Crazy," one rider said. "Her man's lyin' yonder with his brains blowed out, her home's a-fire, and she's thankin' y'all."

"Shut up." Alistair spurred the blood bay.

* * * * *

"You will not set fire to this house!" Maura blocked the path with the white horse.

It was another farmhouse, this one a shotgun-style one-story. No one appeared home. Likely, they had fled. Or were inside ... dead.

"Get the hell out of the way, lady!" A walrus-mustached man with a delicately flowered shirt nudged his stallion forward, drawing an old Dragoon Colt from a saddle scabbard, thumbing back the hammer. The next sound was a click, and the man turned, cursing to see Alistair's Navy pointed at his chest.

"We come here to kill," the man complained. "Your sister got her legs busted at that dungeon in Kansas City. And I hear tell another one of them girls that got kilt ..."

"Remember the girls!" another man shouted.

A third cried out: "Remember Osceola!"

"You heard the colonel's orders," Alistair said. His hand did not waiver. "You threaten her again, I'll kill you."

"Ain't this a pile of shit." Shepherd sprayed tobacco juice on the ground, and let out a mirthless chuckle. "Meacham, look at that place. Ain't nobody home, and any pickin's we'd find there'd be mightily slim. Meacham, Durant, put 'em guns away. We come here to shoot Kansans, not each other. Let's find some to kill."

Cursing bitterly, Meacham lowered the hammer, and slammed the big horse pistol back into the scabbard.

Alistair lowered his Navy, but did not holster it.

They left the farmhouse standing.

* * * * *

Smoke blackened the sky as they rode past South Park.

"Where's the Eldridge?" Shepherd called out without reining in his horse.

"On Massachusetts," Alistair answered.

"And that other hotel?"

"The Johnson?" Alistair tilted his head. "It's on Vermont."

Now Shepherd reined up. He reached inside one of his shirt pockets, and pulled out a crumpled piece of yellow paper. Alistair's stomach again began to heave. He knew what this paper was. When Beans had given Quantrill the list of names, Quantrill had passed it on to John Jarrette to make several copies. Slowly Shepherd unfolded the paper, looked at the names, and asked: "Where's this Capt'n Conor Shea live?"

Alistair would not look at Maura. He simply turned and pointed. "Right down there. About two blocks."

CHAPTER TWENTY

Images, burned forever into Alistair's brain, came out of a nightmare.

A dark-haired farmer sat propped up against a fence, arms stretched out along the lower rail, throat cut from ear to ear.

A boy in his teens lay on the steps of his home, now lost in hungry flames, the back of the boy's shirt smoking.

Two soldiers lay in the ditch, dead, their lips turned upward as if they were sharing an improper joke.

A bushwhacker galloped past them, cutting loose with a Rebel cry, then lifting a bottle to his lips. Behind him he dragged a filthy flag of the United States of America.

A woman walked along the side of the road, away from the roaring flames consuming barns, privies, and homes. Her unblinking eyes stared straight ahead, and from her left hand dangled a rag doll. She did not speak, did not even appear to notice the raiders as they trotted past her.

They rode past another farm. Bushwhackers surrounded the well. Smoke billowed out of the house. Alistair could not see the woman for the crowd of men, but he could hear her. He would always hear her.

"Please, please, for mercy's sake. You've killed my husband. You've killed my oldest son. Spare him. Spare Charles. He's all

I have left. He's just a boy. He's done you no harm. Spare him."

"I spare no Yankee." He recognized Bloody Bill's voice. The revolver's pop made Alistair jump in his saddle.

A woman's unbearable wail followed.

He almost rode too far, but caught his breath, made himself stop thinking about everything going on around him, and reined up in front of a burning three-story mansion.

"Sorry, Oll," he said. "Somebody beat us to the Shea place."

As if he ordained it, the roof crashed down as soon as he finished speaking, startling the tired horses, sending a shower of sparks into the once clear, now vile morning air. Their horses danced, jerking, pawing.

"Well, I hope that bastard's burnin' in there," Shepherd hissed, and spit. "Whoever he was."

"I'm sick of seein' nothin' but farmhouses," Meacham said. "Let's see what's happenin' in town proper."

"Besides," came another, "I ain't et no breakfast."

Shepherd's horse was eager to leave the conflagration. "Suits me," he said, and wheeled the brown around.

Alistair's eyes accidentally found Maura's when he turned the bay. She stared at him, but he could not read her face. Didn't want to, either. She did not thank him, but he had not expected that at all. He glanced at the ruined house, wondering: *Who really lived there?*

* * * * *

They rode away from the base of Mount Oread and into the smoke, turning down Massachusetts. The camp of the Second Kansas Colored was empty of bodies, only trampled tents, scattered clothes, broken boxes remained. Maybe those Negro soldiers had managed to escape, Alistair hoped.

Flames turned the city into Hades. Smoke stung their eyes. They had to keep tight grips on the reins to control their panicked horses.

A young white soldier lay dead in the street. Another body lay on the porch of a home, flames slowly carving a path toward him. Alistair recognized the corpse. It was Card Cardiff, Alun's father, bootless, shot in back of the head, hands bound behind his back.

Behind another building, above the roaring of the inferno, the wails of women and children, a cry came out: "Please don't murder me! Please don't murder me!"

And a callous reply, "No quarter for you redleg sons-of-bitches!" was punctuated with a pistol's report.

Alistair wanted to wake from this nightmare.

Here walked a Jackson County kid named Meyerhoff, hatless and horseless, Starr revolver in his left hand, holding a girl, maybe four years old, in his right arm. The girl's face was covered with soot, streaked from tears. Oddly enough, so was Meyerhoff's. He stopped as they rode by, calling out: "Hey, this little girl can't find her mommy. Have y'all seen her mommy?"

No one answered. Few even dared to look at those poor lost souls.

Through the smoke, dust, and haze, Alistair could see the camp of the white soldiers on New Hampshire. Bodies, a least a dozen, most still in their muslin undergarments, lay dead on the grass. One lay pitched face down in a smoldering cook fire. Beside him squatted a man in a blue embroidered bushwhacker shirt, sipping coffee and chewing on a piece of hardtack. Partisan Rangers walked among the corpse-lined field, drinking whiskey they had liberated from one of the saloons, plundering through knapsacks, saddlebags, trunks, and carpetbags. One of the boys, crazy old Larkin Skaggs, already well in his cups, sat in a camp chair, his boots propped up on a wooden table, singing loudly between gulps from a clay jug.

> John Brown's body lies a-molderin' in the grave,
> John Brown's body lies a-molderin' in the grave,
> But his soul ain't worth a damn.
> Glory, glory, hallelujah,

Glory, glory, hallelujah,
His soul is burnin' in Hell.
Deeper into the chaos they rode.

Some boys had grabbed Dan Palmer in front of his gun shop, had bound his hands to that of another bloodied Kansan. Now the bushwhackers dragged the men toward the burning building.

Oll Shepherd reined up, and the others followed suit, watching. As the Missourians threw the two men through the front door into the raging fire, Shepherd breathed out an oath. Screams of the burning men drowned out all the other hellish sounds. Behind Alistair, one of the boys retched.

The shrieks quickly died.

The murderers laughed, and moved on.

All of which proved too much for Maura. She let out a wail, a groan, slumping in her saddle, almost toppling into the dirt. Meacham eased his mount beside hers, put his arm around her, saying: "There, there, missy. You …"

She recovered instantly, recoiling from his touch, screaming at him, urging her horse forward. "Keep your damned hands off me!" Her words matched the fury on her face, and she kicked the white, moving down to a house that was not burning.

A slender woman followed two Missourians out of her home, begging, pleading. Henry Wilson carried two pillow cases filled with plunder; the other bushwhacker carried a bottle of wine.

Maura met them at the warped gate of the picket fence that surrounded the front yard. "Leave her be!" she barked, and pointed. "Trash, hand back that stuff!"

The man with the wine stared dumbly.

Cursing, Henry Wilson opened the gate.

"I said you're not stealing that. Put it down, I say," Maura insisted.

Henry stopped, suddenly unsure of himself.

"Haven't you done enough?" Maura's voice choked.

Stepping back, Henry Wilson scratched his head, then silently lowered one pillow case, its contents clattering, a volume of Tennyson falling into the dirt. Next he handed the sobbing woman the other pillow case, and, head down, hurried through the gate and down Massachusetts toward the river. The other guerrilla lowered the bottle, and gave it to the woman.

"Beg pardon, lady." He tipped his hat, and followed Henry Wilson down the street.

* * * * *

The Eldridge House was a fury of fire, although one white sheet dangled from an open third-story window, not burning, not blackened, not smoking, not touched. Yet. The courthouse had been consumed. The boys had even torched Danver's Ice Cream Saloon.

Shepherd called out to George Todd, who was mounting his horse, smoking a black cigar, gold chains dangling from his neck: "Where's the colonel?"

Todd hooked a thumb. "City Hotel."

So they cut down to New Hampshire, and approached the Kaw River.

* * * * *

The City Hotel was an oasis. Bushwhackers stood guarding horses, those they had ridden from Missouri, those they had stolen here in Lawrence. Many others sat on one side of the front porch, sipping coffee, smoking cigars, guzzling whiskey. Ladies and children of Lawrence filled the other side of the porch, not speaking. In the front yard, Kansas men sat glumly, heads bowed, wondering if and when they would be shot dead. Many wore only their nightshirts. Others were bootless. A few were bloodied.

Alistair spotted Beans' mount. He swung down, wrapped the

reins of the blood bay around a stump, saw Maura Shea walking through the pathway toward the steps.

A woman, black hair disheveled, skirt ripped, sleeves stained from ash and blood, rose quickly, meeting Maura on the steps. "Traitor!" the woman screeched. "Murderess! Bitch!" She spit in Maura's face, then drew back to strike the stunned girl, but Cole Younger had risen from his rocking chair, and caught the woman's arm.

"There, there, ma'am," Younger said, turning the woman around. "You go find you a shady place to sit and relax."

Glaring, the woman jerked her hand free, but did as ordered.

Maura reached up, tentatively touching the saliva on her nose and cheek, before letting out a tormented wail, and hurrying into the hotel.

Walking past Younger, Alistair wished he were dead.

"It's a grand day of butchery," Younger said, "ain't it?" He patted Alistair's back, and moved back to his rocking chair. Beside him, Frank James sat in brooding silence, face blackened by smoke and rage, reloading a brace of .44 Remingtons.

* * * *

"Alistair! Shepherd!" Quantrill rose, holding a half-filled flute in his left hand, smiling. He sat at the head of the dining room table, a king holding court. "Please, join us. And Miss ..." He snapped his fingers. "Shea, isn't it? Please, do us the honor."

The hotel's owner, Nathan Stone, sat on Quantrill's right, his lovely daughter next to him.

Three Missourians rose, abandoning their seats for Maura, Alistair, and Oll Shepherd.

Flutes were filled by timid waiters, who quickly brought plates of eggs, ham, bacon, potatoes, and biscuits and gravy.

"Nathan and dear Miss Lydia did me a kindness when I lived in Lawrence years back," Quantrill said, nodding at the trembling hosts. "I was deathly ill, but Miss Lydia nursed me back to health. Back then, they knew me as Charley Hart, of course."

"If only she had known," Maura said underneath her breath. She had recovered from the shock, and calmly tilted the flute, pouring the champagne onto the floor.

Quantrill might not have heard her words, but he saw what she did. Sitting again, a forkful of ham in his right hand, he lowered the meat back onto the china plate, and laughed. "You have grit, Miss Shea. All of your Kansas ladies have gumption." He saluted, laughed, and tore into breakfast like a famished man.

Oll Shepherd drained his champagne, then barked out to one of the waiters for coffee. He found Beans Kimbrough and asked: "What about Lane?"

Beans shrugged. "He fled, if he was home." He raised a jeweled sword. "But I got this."

A waiter slid a cup of coffee in front of Shepherd's plate, then hurried back into the kitchen.

"You are a bunch of cowards." Maura's eyes held Alistair's. "All of you."

"Really?" Quantrill beamed. "I've spared this hotel. I've spared all the women and children, even some men. The icehouse isn't burning, either."

"Iffen that ice ain't melted!" slurred a drunken raider at the far end of the table.

Quantrill laughed, and sipped champagne. "You will not find a church burning, dear lady, not even the one belonging to your self-righteous, hypocritical, murdering Methodists."

Confusion masked Maura's face.

"Tell her, Beans," Quantrill commanded.

Hushed voices flowed among the Lawrence citizens.

"Beans."

"That's Beans Kimbrough."

"There's the butcher."

Beans' face hardened, but not from the whispers. He stared

at his plate, started to reach for the flute, but stopped, making himself look at Maura Shea, to mutter: "The pews in that church, ma'am. The church you attend." He took a deep breath. "They come from a church in Osceola."

"Stolen," Quantrill added, "by your fine Lawrence men. And trust me, Miss Shea, those redlegs had no mercy when it came to ransacking Osceola. They burned our houses of God, after they'd looted them."

"Nevada City, too," another bushwhacker muttered.

Maura's head fell. Her fingers balled into fists.

"You're ..." A balding man with his right arm in a bloody sleeve, having heard the whispers, rose from the table. "You are ... Beans ... Kimbrough?"

"The butcher himself," Quantrill said. He raised his glass. "To my most loyal butchers. My eyes and ears. Among the first to join our cause. To Beans Kimbrough. And Alistair Durant."

Glasses clinked, but Alistair had not moved. Couldn't move. He sat paralyzed, sick.

Outside came the sound of another building collapsing. Horses whinnied.

Cole Younger suddenly barged through the door. "Colonel!" he called out, spurs chiming as he made his way to the dining room. "Kennard just come from the lookout. Says there's dust risin' to the east. Lot of dust."

The clock chimed. 9:45. Maybe four hours, only four, had passed since they'd hit Lawrence.

Quantrill's face turned serious, and he rose from his chair, putting his hands on the table. "Shepherd, find Todd, find Anderson and Jarrette. Cole, assemble the men. God help any who is too drunk to ride. We make for Blanton's Bridge." His eyes changed again, and he turned, bowing graciously at the Stones, reaching over, taking Lydia's trembling hand, kissing it. "I wish," Quantrill said softly, "my strongest desire, Miss Lydia, dearest savior, Nathan, my old friend, is that we shall meet again, under circumstances much more convivial than this loathsome war."

Shepherd was already through the door, Younger right behind him. The Missourians scrambled from their seats, wolfing down bacon, slurping the last of their coffee or champagne, knocking over chairs as they fled outside.

Alistair made his legs move, somehow got to his feet. Someone tossed him a hat. It was a tight fit, but he jammed it on his head. Quantrill walked ahead of him, out the door. Beans Kimbrough raced past them, finding his horse, leaping into the saddle, riding down the river road.

On the porch, Quantrill tipped his hat to the ladies, then took in a deep breath, as if the air were fresh, clear, not clouded by smoke, grime, death.

"The ladies of Lawrence are plucky and brave, Alistair," Quantrill said. "But the men ... they are a pack of craven cowards."

A hard hand pushed Alistair aside, and he had to catch himself on a wooden column. Maura Shea sped down the steps. Meacham grabbed her, saying: "Hold on there, honey."

She clawed his face, and he fell backward, stunned, reaching for his revolver.

"Leave it, Meacham," Quantrill ordered.

Maura spun, blinking, her eyes falling on Younger, who had stopped to tighten his saddle girth. "Where did he go?" she yelled.

"Who?"

"John Benedict. I mean ... Beans Kimbrough."

Another bushwhacker answered. "He taken off that way, ma'am."

"God." Maura took a step, hesitated for just a second, then lifting her skirts, she raced through the crowd of stupefied men. "God! God!" After she rounded the corner, a cloud of smoke swallowed her.

Alistair inhaled deeply, let it out slowly, and made a beeline for the blood bay. He knew where Maura was running. Where Beans must be bound.

The Shea house. If it still stood.

CHAPTER TWENTY-ONE

Old Larkin Skaggs was sitting in front of a burning building, holding the reins to his chestnut gelding, lifting a jug to his lips, swaying, saying in a singsong voice: "Let 'em Feds come. I ain't goin' nowhere till I kills me as many as Bloody Bill."

Blackened corpses lined the street.

Dogs wailed mournfully.

Women and children sobbed.

Bushwhackers piled their plunder on the backs of their horses, or onto the horses, mules, or cattle they had stolen.

The heat was oppressive. Alistair spurred the blood bay between privies and buildings ablaze, cut over past Massachusetts, headed up Vermont, coughing, eyes burning again from smoke, cinders, the smell of roasting flesh, of death, of blood. The Methodist church stood untouched, dazed women and boys already carrying corpses inside. Flames consumed the Johnson House. The building next to it by now was smoldering ash and charred timbers. Beyond Eighth Street, Vermont became impassable, so he left the road, following the ravine, then up into the clearing, riding into the next street near a burning home.

The three-story Shea home still stood, though homes next to it were lost amid the wretched black smoke.

He leaped from the saddle before the bay had even stopped, wrapping the reins around the post. The gate had been knocked off its hinges, and horses grazed among the flowers and herbs Mrs. Shea grew in her front yard. He did not see Beans Kimbrough's horse, but saw the fresh scalps dangling from the bridle of a buckskin stallion tethered to a rose bush by the steps. The front door was open. He did not see Maura, either.

Alistair barged inside, glanced at two bushwhackers going through the desk and cabinets inside the parlor, moved through the foyer, and into the dining room. Upstairs, bushwhackers laughed. On her knees by the fireplace, Iris Shea cried, her hands clasped in prayer.

"Please … please … please …"

Conor Shea, in his stockings, pants unbuttoned, suspenders dangling at his sides, a muslin undershirt damp with sweat, his hair unkempt, said nothing. He couldn't talk because of the barrel of the Colt that Bloody Bill Anderson had thrust into his mouth, breaking two front teeth.

"Don't!" Alistair heard himself cry out.

Anderson had just eared back the hammer. He looked, eyes reddened, deadly.

Alistair stopped, caught his breath. "This man is not to be harmed."

"By whose orders?" Anderson did not withdraw the .44.

"Colonel Quantrill."

Iris Shea stopped sobbing. She sank onto her rump, staring in disbelief. "Jim?" Her voice creaked. "Jim Alistair?"

"To hell with Quantrill." Anderson tightened his finger on the trigger. "This man's a damned redleg."

"No, he's not."

A ruction erupted behind Alistair. He heard Maura, but did not dare take his eyes off Conor Shea and Bloody Bill.

John McCorkle raised a sheet of yellow paper. "It says right here …" He dangled the list of names.

"Listen," Alistair said, "this is a good man. He and his wife nursed me back to health when I almost died falling into the river."

"He's a redleg bastard!" another Missourian roared.

"He's no redleg."

"Then explain these!" McCorkle pointed to those Moroccan leather leggings someone had dangled over a plush sofa.

"His son's," Alistair lied. "His son was a redleg, sure, but he was killed at Olathe."

"Then it's time he joined his boy," Anderson whispered, but Alistair stepped closer. He could see Maura in the mirror, one bushwhacker tightly clutching her right arm. To his surprise, he did not see Beans Kimbrough.

Another one of Anderson's murderers knocked Maura's guard's arm with a candlestick. "Leave her be," he said. "This be the lady who helped us find redlegs and jayhawkers."

Then Beans Kimbrough stepped into the frame, coming from the foyer. He had just arrived. Maybe he hadn't come to kill Conor Shea, or maybe, more than likely, Bill Anderson had just beat him here. But so had Maura. He shook his head. There was no time to figure out that mystery.

"Don't kill him," Alistair said, trying to ignore what was going on behind him, focusing on Bloody Bill Anderson and Captain Conor Shea. "He's not to be harmed, according to Colonel Quantrill." He knew it was no use. His right hand dropped for one of the Navy Colts.

"You wanna kill Yanks!" Beans called out behind him, "you'll soon get another chance. Feds are on their way. The colonel's ordered us to ride out. Now. Best save powder and lead, Bill. Chances are you'll have need of it directly."

Alistair and Maura had both misread Beans. He hadn't come here to kill Conor Shea, after all, or had changed his mind. Now Beans was confirming every lie Alistair had been spreading in the Shea home. Except the approaching Yanks. That part was true.

"You're one lucky son-of-a-whore," Anderson hissed, and jerked the barrel out of Shea's mouth, chipping another tooth, then slammed the butt against Shea's head, sending him tripping over his wife, and onto a cabinet. He clutched the back to keep himself from toppling to the rug, but almost pulled the piece of cherry wood down on top of his head.

McCorkle was already gone. Other bushwhackers followed. Lifting her head toward the ceiling, Iris Shea began praying, thanking the Lord for His deliverance. With a glare and an oath, Bill Anderson holstered his Colt, and stormed out of the room, shoving Alistair aside, barking something unintelligible at Beans, but tipping his plumed hat at Maura.

"Let's ride!" Anderson shouted from the foyer. "And be damned quick."

The boys in the bedrooms began descending the staircase.

Alistair stepped toward Mrs. Shea, offering her a hand, which she timidly accepted. He helped her to her feet, then guided her to the sofa. Behind him, Conor Shea righted himself, touched his bleeding forehead, and slowly pulled open a drawer.

"I'm sorry, Missus Shea," Alistair said. "We won't be troubling you any more." He spun around, and tried not to look at Maura, but couldn't help himself. He stopped when he reached her, thinking of something to say, though there were no words. The bushwhackers landed at the bottom of the stairs. Unspeaking, Beans turned to leave.

Maura looked Alistair in the eye. Her face had changed. She looked tired. Old. Down-trodden. Her eyes were rimmed red. Her face filthy.

"Conor!" Mrs. Shea's voice. "No! They'll kill …"

Alistair started to turn, but the explosion roared behind him at the same time a mule punched him hard in the back. Alistair's breath left him, and he felt himself falling past Maura, who screamed. His hands reached out, catching the table before he smashed into it, and he bounced over it, landing face up on the rug. He could not breathe. His hands reached to his chest, and he felt the warmth, the stickiness.

"You damned, thieving, low-life Missouri scum!" Conor Shea

stepped toward him, holding a smoking Kerr revolver in his hand. "And, you, Daughter. You helped these border ruffians. I'll kill …"

He never finished. Alistair heard the roar, knew the two bushwhackers by the stairs, and maybe Beans Kimbrough, had filled their hands.

Conor Shea's muslin undershirt exploded in at least a half dozen splotches of blood, and he staggered back against the cabinet. Another bullet smashed through his left cheek. One caught his Adam's apple. The mirror behind him shattered from balls, crashed to the floor, but Conor Shea stood, if only for a moment. His mouth tried to work, but his eyes rolled into the back of his head. The English-made .45-caliber pistol slipped from his fingers.

Conor Shea fell dead.

Mrs. Shea screamed. She tumbled off the sofa, crawling on her knees to her dead husband. She reached down, sank to her buttocks, lifted his head, blood pooling all around her and his body.

"No …"

Alistair's chest burned with fire. When he coughed, pain intensified. Maura was kneeling beside him, mouth open. Beans ripped open Alistair's shirt, muttering, "Oh, God," and jammed a silk handkerchief into a hole.

The two bushwhackers stood over him. "He's done for," one said.

"No. He'll be all right." For once, panic filled Beans Kimbrough's voice.

Beans pulled Alistair to a seated position. Alistair vomited.

"Get out! Get out of this home. Get out!"

He thought Mrs. Shea was screaming at Beans … at himself … at those bushwhackers who had shot her husband dead. Blinking, he saw her pointing a finger.

"You hussy. You harlot. You're no daughter of mine. You brought them here. Brought them … to … kill … your … father … my …" Into bloody hands, she buried her face, and wept.

"Help me," Beans said to the two bushwhackers.

"Hell," one of the guerrillas said, "he'll be dead in a minute, and the Yanks is a-comin'. Best save your own hide."

The other added: "And leave him to Saint Peter."

Alistair glanced down at his shirt covered with blood. He felt himself being lifted, and he reached out, tears pouring down his face, feeling his bladder release, feeling a terrible panic. He coughed. He thought he saw Maura on his left, helping Beans half drag, half carry him into the morning air. The two other bushwhackers had fled.

"Maura?"

Nothing.

"Beans?"

"Hush up. You're gonna be fine, pard. Just fine."

"Don't tell them," Alistair heard himself wail. "Don't let them know. Don't tell them I was scared, Beans. Don't tell them I was scared."

CHAPTER
TWENTY-TWO

For as long as they could, they kept up with the retreating Missourians, Beans riding double with Maura, pulling Alistair's mount behind them, Alistair's hands lashed to the saddle horn, a rope binding his feet underneath the blood bay's belly. Out of Lawrence and onto the Fort Scott road, they moved, crossing the bridge over the Wakarusa.

The bushwhackers did not ride hard, not at first. They stopped to torch farmhouses and barns. They rode through cornfields, destroying as much of the crops as they could, although they also plucked a few ears, stuffing those into saddlebags and war bags. They killed a preacher in Dunkard. When they hit the town of Brooklyn on the Santa Fe Trail, they burned it, too.

By that time, Quantrill had hand-picked a rear guard of some sixty raiders, and those men rode perhaps a quarter or half mile behind Alistair, Maura, and Beans. Between fleeting bits of consciousness, Alistair thought he heard the popping of revolvers. Finally Alistair heard and felt nothing, until a retching pain jerked him awake.

He blinked, groaning, felt himself being lifted from the saddle. His eyes opened, but he saw only darkness, and, then, to the north, an eerie light, like the sun was setting below the horizon. The sun, however, was also setting to his left.

"What's that?" he asked.

"Lawrence," Maura said.

Then shouts. A pistol shot. And nothing else as he welcomed that cold void that took him deep into an eternal darkness.

* * * * *

When his eyes opened, he saw a sweating, grim-faced black woman with white hair. He could smell her as she worked on his chest. She glanced at him, frowning, and he closed his eyes.

* * * * *

When he awakened next, the Negro woman had changed. She was younger, though her face just as hard. She was white. She was wiping his brow with a damp towel. She was Maura.

Again, the eyes closed.

* * * * *

Voices pulled him out of a deep sleep. He felt as if he were freezing, heard his teeth chattering, felt himself shaking underneath a ton of blankets. The room stopped spinning, and he saw Beans, standing against a sod wall, the door open, light of day streaking into this miserable house. The black woman stood in the doorway, holding a bucket. Beans held cocked revolvers in each hand.

The voices outside grew louder.

"You sure you haven't seen any Missourians?"

"No, sir."

"They burned Lawrence, damn you. And Brooklyn. We still know not how many lives those cowards have taken. And there are two horses in your corral."

He wanted to sit up. That was a voice he'd always recognize. Senator Jim Lane.

"My Navies!" he cried out weakly, and tried to move his arms, to find those .36-caliber revolvers. "My ..."

A hand clasped over his mouth. He looked up, frightened, saw Maura Shea.

"Quiet," she whispered.

"Yes, sir," the voice said outside. "They comes up one night to my trough. I ain't no horse thief. Figured I'd just water and feed these hosses till their owner ..."

"We will relieve you of those horses. Cotton," Lane called out, "go inside that soddy. Make sure this darky isn't lying to us."

"Ain't I a free man?" the voice turned proud, determined. "I recollect you saying that I was free, after you-all fetched me and my wife out of Osceola. Ain't I still free?"

"Of course you are!" Jim Lane barked.

"Then, iffen I be free, don't that mean I get to say who be welcomes in my home, and who ain't?"

Another voice: "Why of all the uppity little nig—"

"That's all, Cotton." Lane again. "Mister McMinn, there is something you can write about in the *Conservative*. We free this man and his wife from a chattel's hard life, provide him with a farm, and this is the thanks we get in return." The voice lowered. "You are sure no one has come by here?"

"Ain't nobody visited us. Just you-all."

"Pray to God you are telling the truth."

Maura's hand lifted off his lips. He could hear saddle leather creaking, the jingling of harness and spurs, sabers, revolvers. Hoofs clopped. The white-haired Negro woman stepped aside, and a man of color entered the home, closing the door.

Beans Kimbrough lowered the hammers on his revolvers, slid them into holsters, and smiled. "You done good, Reginald. Saved a couple of bushwhackers, certain sure. I always knew you loved me, Dilly, but never knowed your husband held me in such high regard." He laughed.

The blackness returned.

* * * * *

No longer did he feel as if he'd freeze to death. The blankets had been removed. Dilly spooned broth into his mouth, but, a few minutes later, he threw it up.

And slept again.

* * * * *

On the fourth try, the broth stayed in his stomach. He even managed to sip some tea Dilly had brewed, but when he tried to sit up, to get out of the bed, the room spun so crazily, he almost passed out.

A few hours later, or maybe it was a couple of days, when he saw Maura carrying the chamber pot through the door, he cried.

This time, he could not fall back asleep.

* * * * *

"How long have we been here?" he asked. Sitting up now, though still on the straw bed in the corner of the one-room sod house.

"Two weeks," Beans answered.

Maura brought another spoonful of broth toward his lips, but he weakly lifted his right hand, stopping her momentarily. "Two weeks? Beans, you need to get out of here."

"Can't." Beans nodded, and Maura made Alistair take the broth.

"But the Yankees ..." Alistair started to say after he had swallowed.

"They've been by here twice, maybe three times," Beans said.

Another spoon. Another question.

"Was that Lane I heard?"

"Which time? He came by the night we left Lawrence, the night we first arrived here. 'Course, I don't think he, nor any of his so-called army, was in no particular hurry to catch up with the boys. Next time, maybe three days later, he came by again. Ol' Reginald stood his ground, though. Else we'd 'a' been goners."

The spoon returned. Alistair felt as if he could taste it now.

"So you brought us to your slaves' place?"

"Providence brought us here. Pure luck. Our horses had played out. Oh, I guess any old home would have done us right, though. Reginald and Dilly knew I'd kill them if they brought any Yanks down upon us. Same as I'd've done any Kansan, black or white." He laughed. "Or maybe God's on our side in this war."

"God," Maura said dryly, "is on no one's side."

* * * * *

Fever returned. He would sweat fiercely, then shake uncontrollably with chills. He couldn't eat, couldn't drink, just lay on that straw bed, wasting away. This time, he figured he was dying, that when he next opened his eyes, he would be facing St. Peter—and he knew what his judgment would be, what he deserved.

This time, he welcomed death.

* * * * *

It was not St. Peter, not Christ, not Satan, not God, but Maura who greeted him.

"Welcome back," she said, and tried to, but couldn't quite, smile.

His hands rested on his stomach, and he managed to move his right one over and cover Maura's hand. "I'm sorry," he said.

She tilted her head, her eyes questioning him, as if she did not understand.

"It's all my fault," he said. "You should go home. Get out of here."

"I have no home," she said. "I'm like you."

"And me." Beans came over, cup of coffee in his hand, and squatted. "We got nobody but Quantrill. How you feeling?"

"Better," he lied.

"You should be dead." He sipped coffee, shaking his head. "Wait till you see the size of that hole under your ribs. Bullet hit you in the back, went all the way through. Criminy, I figured you'd be singing in the sweet hereafter before we even got you out of Miss Maura's home."

"She should go back to Lawrence," he said.

"There is no Lawrence," Beans said. "And don't you remember what her ma told her? Maybe not, almost dead as you was. Her mother kicked her out. And those other ladies of Lawrence ... hell, they all consider Maura one of the boys now, a traitor."

Alistair closed his eyes.

"That's right, pard," Beans said, lowering his voice, his joints creaking as he stood, "you rest. Don't talk so much. You ain't out of the woods yet."

"She should go home," Alistair said before drifting back to sleep.

* * * * *

"Beans," he tried again. "Get out of here. Get back to Missouri."

Behind Beans, Reginald scrubbed a pot while the white-haired woman darned socks. The door was closed, the soddy dark except for the light shining through the open window. Maura sat at the uneven table, staring at a cup of coffee.

"Not till you can ride, pard."

"This doesn't make a lick of sense, Beans. Send Maura home, and you find Quantrill."

Grinning, Beans reached over, squeezed Alistair's hand. "You think I'd leave you?"

Alistair's mouth opened. He didn't know what to say.

"You and the colonel," Beans said. "You're the best friends I got. Hell, you're the only friends I got. Don't you know that? I may be 'Beans the Butcher,' but I'm true to my pards, my pals. I'm—"

Suddenly he stood, right hand gripping the butt of one of his revolvers. Maura also rose, placing both hands on the end of the shaking table, black coffee sloshing over the tin cup's rim. Reginald dropped the pot, and looked up at the roof. With a gasp, Dilly lowered the socks.

Alistair heard it, too, and felt the earth trembling. Hoofs. Bawling cattle. Men's curses. The soddy began quaking. A wooden cross fell off the wall, onto the floor. Dilly rose, clasping the cross dangling from her neck. The ceiling began sprinkling dirt.

"Cattle?" Beans had drawn one of his revolvers. "Buffalo?" Then, hearing the curses of riders, he swore himself.

The dirt began pouring down. A timber creaked.

"We gotta gets out of here!" Reginald yelled.

CHAPTER
TWENTY-THREE

"Come on out of there!" a voice yelled above raining dirt, pounding hoofs, crumbling walls. "Or we bury all of you."

"Don't open that door, Reginald!" Beans drew the second revolver, moved to the window, tried to peer outside, but only managed to cough from all the dust. He had to holster one of the revolvers to wipe his eyes with his bandanna.

Alistair tried to sit up, but the room began spinning again, and he slipped back down. His heart pounded against his throbbing chest. The broth in his stomach roiled. Dirt fell into his hair, over the blankets covering him. He heard horses snorting on the roof. Dirt hit his eyes, blinding him, too.

The air inside the soddy filled with choking dust.

"We know you're in there, you son-of-a-bitch!" another voice commanded. "Throw out your guns. Or we bury you alive."

Beans coughed, managed to shout: "There are two freed coloreds in here! And a white girl!"

"We'll bury them, too!"

A timber brace fell, knocking over the table. A hole appeared in the earthen roof. A steer's leg fell through, the animal bawling and kicking. Even with the new openings in the roof, dust remained too thick to see much of anything other than a few streaks of sunlight.

Reginald and Dilly were dragging away a cupboard, then rolling up a rug—the one patch of color on an earth-toned hut.

"Good God!" Beans covered his mouth with his arm. "A tunnel?"

"No, sir." Reginald had covered his mouth and nose with a bandanna. He moved to Alistair. "But they tells us this place once was part of the Underground Railroad." He paused, coughed, and continued. "They hided coloreds like us in this here hole sometimes. Y'all get in there."

Alistair felt himself being lifted. Reginald scooped him up as if he were a puppy, stepped over the fallen timber. Dilly dropped into the hole, and they eased Alistair down.

"You, too, Mister Benedict," Dilly said. "And you, Miss Maura."

A mound of earth collapsed.

"Cover him," Beans said, smiling.

"You gets in here, Mister Benedict!" Dilly ordered, coughing, spitting out grit, wiping her mouth.

"Cover him! We ain't got much time!"

"But …"

"Damn it, do it, or I'll save them redlegs the trouble and kill you right now!"

Reginald helped Dilly out of the hole. Alistair tried to climb out, but the room blurred, his eyes stung, and then he saw the rug being pulled over him. Fear hit him savagely. First, that he'd be buried alive. Second, that Beans was walking away.

"Beans!"

Beans Kimbrough stopped, turned, his smile bright. "You remember Benedict Kimbrough," he said, "your pard."

The rug covered the hole. Blackness enveloped him. He was in his grave. More dirt fell. By then, Reginald was coughing, as he repositioned the cupboard over the rug and hole. Inside the darkness, Alistair felt hot, yet chilled, all at the same time. His chest burned. He bit his lip to keep from crying out, then couldn't help himself.

"Beans …" All that came out was a hoarse whisper.

A second later, he heard a challenge:

"All right, you Yankee bastards. Here I am! Let's see how many Beans the Butcher can take to hell with him!"

Above the pouring dirt, crashing hoofs, snorting horses, bawling cattle, and Dilly's prayers came a cannonade of gunfire. The last thing Alistair heard, however, was Maura Shea's scream.

CHAPTER
TWENTY-FOUR

BEANS THE BUTCHER IS DEAD!

JOYOUS NEWS OF FEDERAL VICTORY.

DETAILS OF FIGHT AT NEGRO FARM.

MISSOURI RUFFIAN KILLS FOUR
BEFORE HAIL OF LEAD FELLS
THE NOTORIOUS FIEND!

HIS HEAD RETURNED TO LAWRENCE;
HIS BODY DRAGGED BEHIND FOR MILES.

TRAITOROUS WENCH RETURNED TO LAWRENCE,
WHERE SHE IS JAILED.

SEARCH FOR QUANTRILL CONTINUES.

* * * * *

Alistair folded the Topeka newspaper. He couldn't read the article.
Father Finnian Molony reached over, picked up the paper, and

tucked it underneath his arm. The priest frowned, and said: "I am truly sorry for your loss, my son."

"He wasn't a butcher," Alistair said.

"Of course not. And not everyone in Kansas is like Senator Lane, or that girl's father."

Alistair looked up.

The priest smiled. "You spoke a lot in your sleep."

Alistair still wasn't exactly sure how he had got here. Apparently, after the Federals had gunned down Beans Kimbrough, and ridden back to Lawrence, Dilly and Reginald had dug Alistair out of the collapsed soddy. Somehow, they had managed to haul him all the way to Spring Hill, Kansas.

"This paper is a week old," Father Molony said. "More recent news might ease the burden you feel, my son. This girl, Miss Shea, has been released from jail. Her mother has taken her back inside her home. She is now known as a heroine, that she saved many lives during Quantrill's butch—" The priest stopped himself, smiled apologetically, and said: "Raid."

Alistair stared at the wallpaper. "It was butchery, Father."

"Would you like me to hear your confession, my son?"

"I'm not Catholic, Father. I'm Baptist."

"We all have weaknesses."

Alistair smiled. He looked back at the priest, who matched his grin. "I am told that Baptists eat very well." Rising from the rocking chair by Alistair's bed, he moved to the dresser, uncorked a wicker-wrapped bottle, and filled two goblets with red wine. "But we Catholics …" He handed Alistair one of the glasses.

Alistair took a sip, but no more. "Maura did save a lot of lives in Lawrence," he said. "I tried to save her father's life."

"And he shot you for it." Father Molony could be as blunt as a sledgehammer, too. "My son, I have been in Kansas since '56, working for the Underground Railroad. I saw John Brown. I saw border ruffians. I have seen Jennison and Lane and Quantrill and

Shea. Ruthless, vindictive thieves. Some do right. Many others do wrong, but shield themselves with a righteous cause. War brings out the best in some people, an unholiness in others."

"I fall in the latter category." He tried the wine again.

"From what I hear ... well, from what I suspect ... you, too, had a hand in saving lives at Lawrence."

He didn't want to hear any of that. "Father, I am eighteen years old, and I've probably killed twenty men. Maybe more. And I've had a hand in the deaths of hundreds of others."

"Listen ..."

"Some of those men I killed had surrendered, or been captured. They weren't even armed."

"Forgiveness is yours for the asking."

"What about Beans Kimbrough?"

The priest set his goblet on the floor, reached over, gripped Alistair's forearm. "From what Reginald told me when he brought you here, he died to save the lives of you, Miss Shea, Reginald, and Dilly. There is no greater sacrifice."

"Like Jesus?"

Father Molony's eyes twinkled, and, after patting Alistair's arm, he leaned back. "My son, I am not quite sure that I would put Beans Kimbrough up there with the Son of God."

Alistair wanted to laugh, but wasn't sure he remembered how.

They talked some more, about Spring Hill, the mission here, about Clay County, everything and anything other than the war. When Alistair tried to rise out of bed, however, he only managed to spill red wine all over the fine blanket.

Father Molony picked up the empty goblet, and pulled back the blanket, saying: "It's all right."

"It's not all right!" Alistair snapped. "I'm a Partisan Ranger. I ought to be fighting you."

"I'm no soldier. I am not your enemy."

"Neither was Lucy or Cally. You damned Yankees murdered six

girls." Alistair decided to turn his rage back to something he had grown to hate. "You crippled my sister. That's why we came to Lawrence!"

That was a lie. Quantrill had been considering Lawrence for ages. Which was why he had sent Beans and Alistair to spy on the town. The prison collapse might have been the spark, but the fuel had been soaking in coal oil for months.

"That was an accident, a terrible disaster, but not murder."

"It was murder. They collapsed that building on purpose. They killed a girl that I ..." He stopped. Had he loved Lucy Cobb? He couldn't even remember what she looked like, and then he heard her voice in his head.

> True, they tell us wreaths of glory,
> Evermore will deck his brow,
> But this soothes the anguish only,
> Sweeping o'er our heartstrings now.

Only, it wasn't Lucy's voice, but Maura's.

Again, he lashed out at the priest. "There's no wreath of glory for Beans Kimbrough. Nobody's crying for him."

That priest, confound him, would not be provoked into a fight. He wasn't fire-and-brimstone like the New Hope parson. He wasn't easy to rile like Bloody Bill Anderson or George Todd. Instead, the priest again squeezed Alistair's arm.

"My son, you are crying for him now."

TEXAS

CHAPTER TWENTY-FIVE

How he had ever managed that long ride south he would never understand.

Father Molony had given him a horse, a twenty-year-old buckskin mare that had a smooth, if ponderous, gait. Anyway, nobody would suspect him of being a bushwhacker riding that old plug, and she had carried him all the way across Kansas and into Cass County, then south into Bates and Vernon Counties.

Hardly anybody was left in that part of Missouri. He had ridden past burned farms marked only by blackened chimneys. Fields had been abandoned. Sometimes, he would come to an empty home where all that was remained was a dog. Folks had fled in such a hurry, they'd left their hounds behind. Those dogs would wail mournfully as he rode on south.

He never stopped.

General Orders Number Eleven had seen to all this.

After Lawrence, Brigadier General Thomas Ewing had issued the orders, which, for the most part, banished everyone living in Jackson, Cass, and Bates Counties, and part of Vernon County. Oh, from what Alistair had heard, folks who could prove they were loyal to the Union could stay, but, criminy, who could do that? Or, rather, who would do that?

When the war started, Cass County had twenty thousand residents. Now, perhaps six hundred or so lived there.

His own home county, Clay, had been spared. More or less. Word had reached him in Spring Hill—how, Alistair did not know, but figured the Catholic priest had a hand in it—that his father had finally abandoned their farm, tired of Yankees paying visits. Likely, Able Gideon Durant didn't want to get strung up the way Feds had hanged Frank James' stepfather, so he had moved the family in with Grandma Agnes up in Daviess County. Understandably Cally could get better care in Gallatin than in Centerville, Grandma Agnes being a midwife and healer and all.

Daviess County lay too far north, and Alistair wasn't sure he was ready to see his family again. So Alistair had continued south, into Arkansas, then through the Indian Territory, and, finally, took Colbert's Ferry across the Red River and reached Texas.

After Lawrence, Yankees had hit the boys, and poor Missouri families, hard. Orders Number Eleven made things even worse, bringing in more redlegs, who killed old farmers, stole what they could—what hadn't already been stolen—and ran off widows. It was like Lane and Jennison all over again.

Instead of helping the people of Missouri, Quantrill and the boys had retreated to Texas. But not before riling Kansans and Federals even more in October by striking Baxter Springs, Kansas. The boys had tried assaulting a little post there called Fort Blair, mostly log cabins and earthen walls, but the Feds had a cannon, so they had managed to hold off the boys. Another bunch of Yankees came in from Fort Scott, however, and Quantrill had caught those by surprise, leaving more than one hundred dead, including the band.

That's what Alistair thought about when he heard a horn blaring in the camp along Mineral Creek, less than twenty miles northwest of Sherman. Oll Shepherd stood as sentry, sipping corn liquor from a jug, and aimed a Dragoon at Alistair's head when he eased the buckskin, by then worn to a nubbin, down the woods road.

Alistair reined up, staring, not speaking.

The .44's barrel dropped like an anvil to Shepherd's side. "I be damned," Shepherd said. "Durant, be that you? We figured you dead like Larkin Skaggs."

Larkins Skaggs, Father Molony had informed Alistair, had been too drunk to ride off with Quantrill's men. Federals, or maybe Lawrence citizens, had cut him down, the only bushwhacker killed during the raid.

Replied Alistair: "Almost."

"Reckon you heard about Beans." Shepherd held up the jug toward Alistair.

"Yeah." Ignoring Shepherd's offering, Alistair eased the old mare past him, and headed toward the picket line of horses.

* * * * *

He tethered his horse, leaving the saddle and blanket drying underneath an elm, then making his way into camp, an ugly conglomeration of tents, picket houses, shacks, huts, trash, and drunks. Whoever had been tooting that horn had stopped. The camp almost fell quiet, except for a heated exchange in front of a log cabin, the only structure of any substance in the entire compound. Alistair paused, blinking. One of the men yelling, shouting the loudest, in fact, was Quantrill. The other man, George Todd, turned on his heel, right hand gripping the butt of a revolver, and stormed away.

Quantrill cursed him, then cursed another man who had just walked from the shadows and stood in front of the cabin.

"I'll be happy to accommodate you, *sir*." It was Bloody Bill Anderson, putting as much contempt into the *sir* as he could. He tossed a glove at the colonel's feet

"You ain't no leader," Anderson said. "You ain't nothin'. Get back inside with your whore. Or make your play."

Quantrill started for his revolver, but stopped, staring, maybe sweating. From this distance, Alistair couldn't really see.

"I will discipline you later, Anderson." The door slammed shut behind Quantrill, and, laughing, Anderson bent over for his glove.

Which is when a large hand pounded Alistair's back and almost doubled him over. He groaned, bending, grasping at his ribs, feeling the old wound throb.

"Alistair Durant, by thunder, you do these old eyes a world … Aw, hell, I'm sorry, kid." Cole Younger eased Alistair up, guided him to a cook fire in front of two huts and a stained, ripped tent. "Boys," Younger said, "look who has returned from Purgatory."

Frank James grinned—it looked like the first time he'd smiled in months—and filled a tin cup with coffee. Younger eased Alistair onto a stump, still mumbling apologies, taking the cup Frank James held, and shoving it into Alistair's hand.

"I can sweeten that up for you," Younger said.

Alistair tasted the chicory. "No," he said, "this is fine."

"Where you been?" Frank James asked.

Alistair drank more. "Almost to hell," he said. "What's been going on around here?"

"Welcome to hell." Younger sank beside Alistair, making himself a cup of coffee. "You know about Beans?"

"Yeah."

Silence.

"Well?"

When no one said anything, Alistair said: "I see the temperaments of Todd and Bloody Bill haven't changed." He was trying to make a joke, but no one laughed.

Frank James spit tobacco juice into the fire. "Quantrill and Bloody Bill's been going at each other. Todd, too. Things been turning bad since …" "Lawrence" went unspoken.

"My bet is we'll be splitting up before long," Younger said. "Some with Quantrill. Some with Anderson. Some with ... whoever."

Alistair looked at a kid in a bushwhacker shirt staring silently over the flames, wetting his lips, wondering if he should join the conversation. Jim Cummins came over and sat across the fire, but said nothing, nursing a bottle of rye. Alistair looked across the camp at other fires, other faces. "Where's McCoy?" he asked.

Younger shook his head.

"Kennard?"

"He's dead, too." Frank James shifted the tobacco to his other cheek.

"But you recognize this kid?" Younger leaped up, grabbing the quiet boy's arm, pulling him to his feet, rushing him closer to Alistair as if he needed spectacles.

Alistair studied the face. It did look familiar, but he couldn't place it.

"Tell him who you are," Younger said.

The kid spoke: "Darius Kimbrough."

Alistair set the cup down. He tried to swallow, but couldn't. "What are ...?"

"Yankees killed my brother," Darius said. "They called him a butcher. They cut off his head. We don't even know where he's buried. There's no monument over my brother's grave!"

Frank James spit again. "He made his monument while he lived. Like a lot of our boys."

Darius Kimbrough straightened. "I aim to kill as many Yankees as I can. I'll avenge my brother."

CHAPTER
TWENTY-SIX

Alistair couldn't finish the chicory. Couldn't say hardly a word. He rose, stiffly, his chest still hurting, and walked toward the cabin.

"Where you going?" Cole Younger called out.

"Best tell the colonel I'm here," he said.

"What for?" Cummins slurred bitterly.

* * * * *

The cabin door was open, and Quantrill was outside again, holding a goblet of wine in one hand, shaking the other at Lieutenant William Gregg. "And where do you think you'll be going, Mister Gregg?"

"Shelby maybe. Some other command. I don't want to be shot in the back." His eyes narrowed. "By my own men. Or my commanding officer."

"Then be gone, and good riddance." Wine sloshed across Quantrill's shirt front, and he flung the goblet to the carpet of pine needles on the ground. "I …" He saw Alistair then, and raced past Gregg, running, smiling, his eyes even welling with tears. He stopped, breathing heavily, then reached out and pulled Alistair to him, kissing both cheeks, then pushing Alistair back an arm's length, staring.

"I feared you dead."

"No, sir."

"By Jehovah, you are a blessing to a weary heart. Come!" He put his arm around Alistair, and guided him past William Gregg, who did not speak, nor was spoken to, and into the cabin. The door shut behind him, and Alistair stared at the lavish plunder.

Oh, the cabin was only one large room, but a four-poster canopied bed stood in one corner. There were trunks, cabinets, even a lawyer's bookcase filled with volumes, the top covered with wine and champagne bottles, whiskey bottles, crystal glasses, china, silver. In the center, a woman in a blue satin dress sat at a cherry table covered with china, crystal, and plenty of food. Woman? Hell, she was barely in her teens.

"Alistair Durant, meet Kate Clarke, my wife."

She glanced at him timidly, then stared at the carrots and venison on her plate. She looked like a Missouri farm girl all dolled up.

"Come, sit, dear lad, sit." Quantrill dragged a chair across the earthen-packed floor to the table, waited until Alistair was seated, then looked around. "Damnation, this bottle of wine is empty." He hurried to a cupboard, looked, grabbed a china cup, filled it with something from a crystal decanter, brought it over, and set it in front of Alistair. "Eat. Eat. You are thin as a sapling, and pale as cotton. Drink. This is a most excellent brandy. Well, the best one can find in a place devoid of civilization."

Alistair glanced around the cabin. "You seem to have done all right," he said.

Laughing, Quantrill slipped into his plush chair. The girl, Kate Clarke, still stared at her food, head bowed, unmoving.

"Hard times have befallen our lot," Quantrill said, filling a tumbler with brandy. "Hard times, indeed. Some are near mutiny. So it is divine intervention that you arrive at this time, Alistair. I need loyal men. Men who do their duty to me. Like you have always done. Like Beans Kimbrough, God rest his martyred soul." Quantrill sipped brandy himself, then laughed. "But I will fight without Todd and Gregg and Anderson. I have not forgotten that those Kansas scoundrels killed my arthritic brother Franklin. I shall never forget how they treated Beans the Butcher Kimbrough in death. I had ..."

Alistair lowered the cup. "I thought his name was Thomas Henry?"

Quantrill stopped, stared.

"Your brother," Alistair explained. "The one the jayhawkers killed."

The colonel's eyes changed. "Thomas Henry was my father's name. I would not ever mourn his passing. My father, that pathetic ..." He stopped himself, smiled. "You are mistaken, lad. My brother's name is ... *was* ... Franklin. Drink. Drink and eat. We have much to discuss."

Maybe. Alistair couldn't be certain. These days, he hardly recalled his own name. He brought the china cup to his lips, started to taste the brandy, then lowered it. He stared, and his hand started shaking. He set the cup on the linen tablecloth. His heart pounded.

"What is it, lad? Are you all right?" Quantrill sprang to his feet, rushing to Alistair's side.

"Did ...?" He tried to think. Thoughts swarmed through his head in all directions. "Did Darius bring this?" His chin pointed at the cup.

"Darius? What? Who? Are you sure you're all right?"

Alistair pointed at the cup. "Where did you get this?"

"This cup? Thunderation, boy." Quantrill laughed. "From a damnyankee, no less. Lawrence, perhaps. I disremember."

Alistair reached out, saw his hand shaking, and fingered the small cup, tracing the gold rim. The laugh that came coughing out held no joy, and he looked up, tears now filling his own eyes, and he heard himself saying, his voice cracking: "You are a damned liar."

Quantrill stepped back, his face dropping, his right hand reaching for that huge pistol tucked inside his sash.

"You stole that from Beans Kimbrough's house." Alistair stood. "Remember? After Wilson's Creek."

"I freed this from a redleg's home in Baxter Springs!"

Alistair rose, shaking his head. "No." Though it could have been. Hell, it wasn't like the Kimbroughs were the only wealthy folks who owned gold-rimmed china. He was guessing. But, no, his gut told him the truth.

"It came from Beans Kimbrough's house."

"What if it did?" Quantrill spun, found his own brandy, tried to drink, but his hand shook, too. He threw the glass against the fireplace, where it shattered. "His father was no patriot to our cause. He was a coward and a traitor. Worse than that miserable reprobate who I unfortunately called my own father."

Alistair took a step.

"What are you doing?"

"Leaving," he said.

Quantrill moved to block his path. "You will not, I say. Sit. Drink. Please, let us not quarrel." When Alistair refused to obey, the colonel exploded. "Look at you! In poor man's clothing. You do not even don a bushwhacker shirt. Have you forgotten all I have done for you, Durant? I showed you Richmond. I showed you Saint Louis. I bought you the finest clothes. I made you what you are. I taught you ..."

It was too much. Alistair shoved Quantrill aside, headed for the door.

"Where are you going?"

Alistair pulled the latch string, pushed the door open.

"Don't you turn your back on me, you insolent bas—"

Alistair spun, saw Quantrill bringing the LeMat from his sash, but the Navy leaped into Alistair's own hand, and he had the hammer eared back, the barrel level, before Quantrill had his gun up.

In the corner of his eye, Alistair spotted Kate Clarke looking up. She appeared to be smiling.

"Toss that gun on the table," Alistair said in a deadly whisper. "If you don't, I'll kill you. And killing's one thing you've taught me how to do too well."

Paling, Quantrill moved to the table, dropped the gun beside a plate of fried chicken, and stepped away, hands at his side.

"I'm leaving," Alistair said. "But there's something I must do first. And if you stick your head outside that door before morning, I'll kill you."

"Alistair," Quantrill begged. Tears rolled down his cheeks.

Alistair backed outside, slamming the door shut.

"To hell with you, Alistair Durant!" Quantrill screamed at the door, but he made no move to come outside.

* * * * *

He moved methodically back toward the cook fire. What did it matter? Truly matter? William Quantrill had stolen a china mug—something else, too, what was it? Silverware? Yeah, silverware. Who cared. And maybe Beans' father had been a coward. Maybe he had tried to stay out of the war. Did it matter? Was Quantrill's brother's name Thomas Henry or Franklin? Who cared? Had he really been killed by jayhawkers, or was that another lie? Did Quantrill even have a brother? No, nothing mattered. Not really.

Beans Kimbrough had called Quantrill one of his only friends. Would he have been so loyal had he known that Quantrill had stolen from his own home, where he had spent the night as a guest? Honestly Alistair didn't know the answer. Maybe he just wanted an excuse to leave, to quit Quantrill. Since he'd started riding as a Partisan Ranger, he had felt dirty. Now, he felt used. Betrayed.

No, all that mattered was Alistair's conscience, his soul.

He stepped over the log, and slammed a fist into Darius Kimbrough's face. Beans' kid brother, who had been standing, sharing a joke with Jim Cummins, dropped. Frank James and Cole Younger stepped up, eased away from the fire.

In a neighboring camp, someone called out excitedly: "Fight!"

Darius came up, wiping his nose, starting for the Starr

revolver in his waistband, but Alistair hit him again, and, when Darius folded, Alistair jerked the .36 out, quickly tossed it over a stump. Then slammed a fist into the kid's temple.

"You're going home," Alistair said. "Your mother needs you. Especially now."

The kid was on hands and knees, crawling, spitting blood and snot, trying to stand. Alistair's wound throbbed, but he ignored it, and kicked Darius in the ribs. The boy rolled over, curling up into a ball.

"You didn't even like your brother."

"I did ..."

Alistair reached down, grabbed Darius' hair, jerked up his head, slammed it into the dirt. "You're going home." He was sweating, his heart pounding, his breath ragged. "This isn't ... starting again. You get ... to your horse ... right now. You saddle up. You ride. Back to ... Osceola."

"But ..."

He kicked the kid in the thigh. Darius cried out. "Are you going?" Alistair roared. "Or do I ... carry you back?" He moved as if to strike the kid again.

"Don't hit me!" Darius wailed. "I'm going. I'm going."

* * * * *

After Darius Kimbrough had filled his war bag, saddled his dun, and ridden out of camp, Alistair sat by the fire again, coffee cup in his hand, watching the flames, seeing Lawrence burning again.

"What come over you?" Jim Cummins asked. "To give that boy such a whuppin'?"

Alistair saw the Johnson House. He saw the gun shop. He saw the Eldridge. "I'm leaving, too," he said to no one in particular.

"With Bloody Bill?" Cole Younger asked.

His head shook. "I don't know. Sibley, maybe. Somewhere."

"You're welcome to ride with me, Durant," William Gregg said. "My horse is ready. I leave in a few minutes."

"Regular army, eh?" Frank James chuckled.

Alistair looked up. "Why don't y'all come with us?"

Frank's laughter died, and he spit again. Jim Cummins decided to finish his rye.

"I know something's come betwixt you and the colonel, kid." Cole Younger spoke softly. "The reason ain't none of our business. But I reckon we've floated our stick with the colonel all this time. He's got his faults, but ..." Younger shrugged.

"It's a hell of a war," Jim Cummins said after a lengthy silence, just to say something.

* * * * *

It was midnight when he saddled the black gelding. A fine horse, too good for the even trade Frank James had made for the buckskin, but Alistair knew better than to argue with Frank James. He shook Cole Younger's hand, then Frank James', even Jim Cummins'.

"You ready?" William Gregg was already in the saddle.

Alistair swung up. The black fought the bit, wanting to run. Soon Alistair would give the horse plenty of rein.

"It's a hell of a war," Jim Cummins, well in his cups, said again.

Alistair tipped the brim of his hat. William Gregg eased his horse out of the picket. Instead of returning to the woods road, he moved through camp, and Alistair followed. They would steer clear of roads, of people, of towns, until they had reached Arkansas, where they would try to find Jo Shelby or Sterling Price or anybody in a gray or butternut uniform. Anyone who was not commanding an outfit of Partisan Rangers.

Gregg rode with a revolver in his right hand, the hammer eared back. For now, until they were out of camp, Alistair did the same.

The path they took led them straight past Quantrill's cabin. From inside, Alistair heard the sounds of a man sobbing, and he almost lost his resolve. But he kept riding out of the camp's light, into the darkness, through the trees.

"A hell of a war," he heard himself whisper.

HIGGINSVILLE

EPILOGUE

Every year about this time, they'd flock to the Confederate Soldiers Home of Missouri like mosquitoes. Pesky little ink-slingers, wanting to hear all about Lawrence. Wanting some scoop. To learn one more tidbit about William Quantrill or Bloody Bill Anderson—God's truth or shameless falsehood, it mattered not. This year, 1923, being one of those big anniversaries, Alistair Durant knew they'd come out in droves, and they had. He had told all of them: "Go to hell."

Which he was about to tell this curly-haired gent in a straw hat and high-waist jacket, till the reporter said he came from the *Osceola Tribune.*

Craning his head, Alistair looked the bespectacled young man in the face, and said: "I didn't think Osceola had a newspaper."

"It's small." The kid smiled. Tried to, anyway, nervous as he was. "But one of the best papers in the state."

Missouri brag.

Alistair snorted, and went back to watching the birds and the trees and looking at the tombstones. He sat on a bench, in the shade, near the little chapel, with a good view of the cemetery. That boneyard kept growing. He pointed.

"I'll be buried there, too." He nodded in satisfaction. "One day."

To his left, Henry Wilson said: "You're too ornery to die, Durant. Hell, you'll even outlive Comrade Cummins."

To his right, Jim Cummins spit tobacco juice, and stroked the hair of his pet raccoon. "That'll be the day," he said.

The reporter cleared his throat. "Can I talk to you gentlemen?" His voice creaked nervously. "About Lawrence."

"Never been there." Jim Cummins chortled.

"And I promised that good-lookin' gal from the *Star* that I'd give her an exclusive," Henry Wilson said. "Wouldn't say nothin' else to nobody."

"Looks like it's up to you, Durant," Cummins said.

Turning, staring at the ink-slinger, Alistair asked: "Why do you always wanna know about Lawrence? Why not Osceola? Or Nevada City?"

The reporter fumbled to retrieve his notebook and pencil from his coat pocket. "Well … Lawrence sells newspapers. Especially this year, sixty years ago and all. And we're doing a story on Osceola, too. In conjunction with your reunion. But my assignment is Lawrence. And … er … Quantrill … and … er … Well, can I ask you about Lawrence?"

"No." Alistair looked at the graveyard. He had been to another funeral just last week.

"Will you be attending this year's reunion of Quantrill's band?"

"He has," Cummins answered for him, "since the first one back in '98."

"Not so many of us left these days, though," Henry Wilson added.

The first reunion of Quantrill's survivors had been held at Blue Springs. They had been meeting one weekend in September ever since, though death kept depleting the number of survivors. Even Frank James and Cole Younger were gone now. Of old age.

"What did Jesse James do at Lawrence?" the reporter asked.

"Killed fifty men," Henry Wilson lied.

"Nah, it was only forty-seven," Cummins added.

Alistair shook his head, decided to talk a little. "They're funning you, kid. Jesse wasn't even there."

Jesse had joined up after Alistair had left Quantrill in Texas, in the spring of 1864, but wound up fighting mostly with Bloody Bill. He'd learned well, too. After the war, he, brother Frank, and Cole Younger had made quite the name for themselves, robbing banks, trains, before Jesse had been shot dead in 1882. During the late 1860s and early 1870s, Alistair would let the outlaws sleep in his barn, even swap horses with them, but that was because of a loyalty to Frank and Cole, not Jesse. He had barely known Jesse.

Tired of staring at the backs of the bushwhackers' heads, the reporter moved around. Looking down at Alistair, he asked: "You are Alistair Durant, aren't you?"

He stared at the reporter. "What of it?"

"They say you saved a lot of Kansans' lives that day. In Lawrence."

"Hell, no," Jim Cummins said. "He killed all seven hundred that day."

Added Henry Wilson: "Exceptin' the fifty Jesse shot dead."

Seven hundred? Not hardly. More like one-fifty, maybe two hundred. Still a massacre. What had Cole called it? "A grand day of butchery."

"Who says I saved lives?" Alistair tried to push off the bench, but it was too damned hot, and he was too damned tired, to move. Till the nurses came for them.

"Maura Shea Morgan, the Florence Nightingale of Lawrence."

Henry Wilson wiped his nose. "Hear her son's got a good chance of becomin' lieutenant governor of Kansas. She was a good-lookin' petticoat, I tell you that. Wonder if she still looks so fine."

"Don't get yourself lathered up, ol' comrade," Jim Cummins said.

"You interviewed Maura?" Alistair asked.

"Yes. At her home in Manhattan."

Alistair reached inside his shirt, felt the scar underneath his ribs.

"I had a pillowcase full of plunder," Henry Wilson was saying, "and she come up to me, and made me hand it back to this sobbin' woman. That was in Lawrence." He quickly shot the reporter a nervous stare. "But I didn't kill nobody in Lawrence. Nobody at all."

"Only 'cause Durant killed 'em all," Jim Cummins said, and chuckled. The raccoon on his lap growled.

"I thought I was giving this interview!" Alistair snapped.

"Well, hell, tell the boy somethin'," Henry Wilson muttered.

"Something good," Jim Cummins said.

"Tell me about Quantrill." The reporter scribbled in his notebook, and flipped to a new page.

William Clarke Quantrill. Friend and mentor. Manipulator and opportunist. Turns out, he hadn't been born in Kentucky, but hailed from Ohio, had even ridden with Yankees in Kansas before siding with the Confederacy. Somehow, despite the discontent in Texas during the winter of 1863–64, he had managed to keep some semblance of a command. George Todd and Bloody Bill Anderson had pulled out, struck out on their own, only to be shot down by Federals in the fall of 1864. Quantrill almost survived the war. Did live, in fact, after the regular Confederate generals had started to surrender, only to be shot down in 1865.

Over those long decades, many had formulated theories on what Quantrill was planning. That he was running for his life. That he wanted to save his men, hoped they would have a better chance of not being executed as bushwhackers if they surrendered with a regular Rebel Army back east somewhere. That he was bound for Washington to kill as many Yankee leaders as possible. That he wanted to lend his capable services to Robert E. Lee. You could even find a few who thought he wasn't dead at all, that there was no way in hell a Yankee could have ever captured and killed William Clarke Quantrill.

But he was dead. Alistair knew that. His group—Frank James had been with him, but by then Quantrill's ranks had thinned down to maybe twenty raiders—had been ambushed, and Quantrill caught a ball in his spine, paralyzing him from the shoulders down. He had dropped facedown in the mud, his assailants stealing his boots, his watch, his dignity. An ignoble end. Or maybe a fitting one. Quantrill withered away for almost a month, dying in Louisville on June 6, 1865.

He was twenty-seven years old.

Some of Quantrill's boys, like Arch Clements and Oll Shepherd, were gunned down after the war. Clell Miller died riding with the James-Younger gang. Others, like Henry Wilson, Jim Cummins, and even Alistair Durant, merely got old.

"Quantrill was the best by-god general in the whole Confederate Army," Jim Cummins said.

Henry Wilson added: "He was a horse's ass."

Alistair shook his head. He gave up on trying to keep those two old codgers quiet.

The reporter paused to wipe his sweaty brow. A cardinal landed on a hedge, and began singing. The raccoon began to snore. Or maybe it was Jim Cummins.

"Quantrill?" the kid prodded.

"Everything's been written about Quantrill that can be written," Alistair said.

The reporter tried another approach. "You left Quantrill, though? Right? Was that because of Lawrence?"

He thought about telling the kid to go to hell, but said: "Left for my own ... *private*, reasons." He was going to stop there, but, instead, kept talking. "Joined up with Jo Shelby around Clarendon, Arkansas, in spring or summer of '64. When the war ended, Jo Shelby took some troops south to Mexico. Planned to fight for Maximilian, but I'd had my fill of war. I went home."

"What did you do after the war, sir?"

"Went back to farming," he answered, the words flowing comfortably all of a sudden. "Wasn't much else I could do, what with carpetbaggers running the state, and all. Met a woman at New Hope. That was my church. I'm Baptist, you see. Married her in '71. Lost her in '09. But we had a good life. I have no complaints. Gave my oldest boy the farm, moved into the Home here back in July of '11. My kids come to see me on Sundays. Most Sundays, anyhow. And grandkids. They don't ask impertinent questions about what I did during the war."

He looked left, then right. Cummins' and Wilson's heads had tilted forward. They were sleeping. Or faking it.

"From what I've heard and read," the reporter said, "you were driven to become a bushwhacker."

"We all claimed that." Taciturn again.

"Kansans and Missourians hated each other."

"Many still do."

"Do you?"

"Hate Kansans?" He snorted, and the words spilled out freely. "A few years before he died, Frank James got up at one of our reunions, and he says that it was time to forgive. Says he ... 'I believe that if we expect to be forgiven, we must forgive. They did some very bad things on the other side, but we did, too.' Remember it like it was just the other day."

He let the reporter finish scribbling. The kid looked up, wiped his brow again. "Frank James really said that?"

"Sure, 'bout ten years back."

"But have you forgiven?"

"Kansans?" He laughed. "Sure. That was a hell of a war, kid. No glory. No wreaths of glory, not really, but I suspect all wars are like that." He leaned forward. "But this was nothing like that thing over in Europe a few years back. We were fighting the Huns in that one. Back then, we were fighting each other. They call it 'Civil War,' but, trust me, there wasn't one thing *civil* about it. I done plenty of wickedness during the war. I'm not proud of anything I did. Didn't do one good thing. I was a kid, though. Cole Younger once said it's pretty easy to turn a boy, in his teens or just beginning his twenties, into a killer. Just give him a revolver and a cause and a leader who can make him forget his conscience. That was me. No, I don't begrudge any Kansans."

Well, he had done a few skips and hops, and shouted a huzzah or two in 1866, upon hearing that Senator Jim Lane had blown his brains out.

"And what about Beans the Butcher Kimbrough?"

So it had finally come back to Beans. The cardinal took flight, disappearing in the woods beyond the cemetery. Alistair looked at the graveyard, the wilted flowers by the marble headstones, a few flags—American and Rebel—being swallowed by the tall grass that desperately needed mowing.

He was tired of talking. Hadn't spoken so many words since the Quantrill reunion in 1914, when Frank and Cole were still living. He sat straight again. "Did you ask Maura ... Missus Morgan, I mean ... about him?"

The reporter studied Alistair's face before answering deliberately. "She said he never mistreated her in any way when she rode out of Lawrence with him. She said he died as a soldier, fighting for his cause. She bore him no animosity. And as I said, she spoke highly of you."

He listened to the other birds, the wind rustling through the trees overhead.

"Beans Kimbrough," the reporter said. "came from Osceola ..."

"His name was Benedict," Alistair said.

"Yes. Yes. I know. There's no monument to him, and many in Osceola consider him a hero, much as they still admire Bloody Bill Anderson and William Quantrill and Jo Shelby and ..."

"Yeah." Alistair waved his hand. "Plenty of Confederate heroes. I reckon we have enough. Kimbrough wouldn't want some monument. He's remembered. And Frank James said something else, it was during the war, he said ... 'He made his monument while he lived.'"

The reporter wrote that down, then said: "A group in Osceola wanted to fund and commission a statue of Beans the Butcher, but my boss, our publisher, he wrote a scathing editorial, pretty much saying the same thing you just said, that we need not stir up animosity, that the war is over, and we need to forget it. And he's an Osceola native, my editor. He's old, too, almost as old as …" He stopped himself, smiled sheepishly, and said: "Anyway, he was in Osceola when Union soldiers burned it. Not only that, his last name is Kimbrough. One would think that …"

Alistair looked up. "Kimbrough?"

"Yes, sir. Darius Kimbrough."

Lips turning upward in a smile, Alistair crossed his legs, shook his head, and whispered: "I don't know. Maybe I did one thing good during the war, after all."

The ink-slinger tried to ask another question, begging Alistair to repeat what he had just said, that he hadn't quite caught all of that, but the nurses had come to the rescue, shooing away the reporter. They tried to load Cummins, Wilson, and Alistair into those confounded wheelchairs, waking up Cummins' pet raccoon, which leaped down, startling one of the nurses so badly she fell onto her backside. Snarling, the raccoon climbed up a tree. Cummins cursed, started crying for his pet. Henry Wilson pinched one of the nurse's bottoms, and she slapped his face. Another nurse screamed at the raccoon, then at Cummins. The reporter tried to shout one last question, but Alistair Durant was laughing too hard to hear.

It was good to be alive. It was good to have forgiven, and to have been forgiven.

THE END

AUTHOR'S NOTE

This is a work of historical fiction, and since my protagonists are Missouri-born, their thoughts and actions are what I think would be appropriate for a Missouri-born teenager caught up in those horrid War between the States years. According to contemporary accounts, most bushwhackers believed that the collapse of the women's "prison" in Kansas City was premeditated murder. Some people still regard it as such, despite solid historical evidence citing the cause of the tragedy as this: Union guards unintentionally undermined the structure by tunneling to reach the cells of prostitutes also imprisoned there.

For the purpose of narrative, I did lengthen the time the girls were imprisoned in Kansas City, and, according to some sources, the "spy period" of Quantrill's men in Lawrence. Other events are either loosely based on actual events or solidly grounded in historical record.

Alistair Durant and Beans Kimbrough are fictional composites of Missourians who rode with William Quantrill. Maura Shea is loosely based on Lawrence resident Sallie Young, who was captured by Quantrill's raiders and originally despised (and jailed) as a traitor before being exonerated as a true heroine. Many other characters— Quantrill, Bill Anderson, Jim Cummins, Frank James, Jim Lane, George Todd, and Cole Younger among them—were actual people.

Much appreciation goes to the staffs at the Bushwhackers Museum in Nevada City, Missouri; Confederate Memorial State Historic Park in Higginsville, Missouri; Jesse James Farm and Museum in Kearney, Missouri; Lawrence (Kansas) Convention and Visitors Bureau; Missouri Valley Special Collections at the Kansas City Public Library; and Watkins Community Museum in Lawrence, Kansas. I must also thank Max McCoy of Emporia, Kansas, for recommending several sources.

William Quantrill and the border wars have generated scores of books, some reliable, many not. Among the best sources I found during my research were: *Gray Ghosts of the Confederacy* (Louisiana State University Press, 1958) by Richard S. Brownlee; *Bloody Bill Anderson: The Short, Savage Life of a Civil War Guerrilla* (Stackpole, 1998) by Albert Castel and Thomas Goodrich; *Civil War on the Missouri-Kansas Border* (Pelican, 2006) by Donald L. Gilmore; *Bloody Dawn: The Story of the Lawrence Massacre* (Kent State University Press, 1991) and *Black Flag: Guerrilla Warfare on the Western Border, 1861–1865* (Indiana University Press, 1995), both by Thomas Goodrich; *The Devil Knows How to Ride: The True Story of William Clarke Quantrill and His Confederate Raiders* (Random House, 1996) by Edward R. Leslie; *Reminiscences of Quantrell's* [sic] *Raid upon the City of Lawrence, Kansas,* (Isaac P. Moore, 1897) edited by John Shea; *"The Burning" of Osceola, Missouri,* (self-published, 2009) written and compiled by Richard F. Sunderwirth; and *Frank and Jesse James: The Story Behind the Legend* (Cumberland House, 2000) by Ted P. Yeatman. And although you can't believe most of what they said, *The Story of Cole Younger by Himself* (Minnesota Historical Society Press, 2000) and *Three Years with Quantrill: A True Story Told by His Scout John McCorkle* (University of Oklahoma Press, 1992) written by O. S. Barton were good for flavor.

These are excellent sources to learn more about the Civil War years in Missouri and Kansas, and the Lawrence raid.

Johnny D. Boggs
Santa Fe, New Mexico

ABOUT THE AUTHOR

Johnny D. Boggs has worked cattle, shot rapids in a canoe, hiked across mountains and deserts, traipsed around ghost towns, and spent hours poring over microfilm in library archives—all in the name of finding a good story. He's also one of the few Western writers to have won six Spur Awards from Western Writers of America (for his novels, *Camp Ford*, in 2006, *Doubtful Cañon*, in 2008, and *Hard Winter* in 2010, *Legacy of a Lawman*, *West Texas Kill*, both in 2012, and his short story, "A Piano at Dead Man's Crossing", in 2002 and the Western Heritage Wrangler Award from the National Cowboy and Western Heritage Museum (for his novel, *Spark on the Prairie: The Trial of the Kiowa Chiefs*, in 2004). A native of South Carolina, Boggs spent almost fifteen years in Texas as a journalist at the *Dallas Times Herald* and *Fort Worth Star-Telegram* before moving to New Mexico in 1998 to concentrate full time on his novels. Author of dozens of published short stories, he has also written for more than fifty newspapers and magazines, and is a frequent contributor to *Boys' Life* and *True West*. His Western novels cover a wide range. *The Lonesome Chisholm Trail* (Five Star Westerns, 2000) is an authentic cattle-drive story, while *Lonely Trumpet* (Five Star Westerns, 2002) is an historical novel about the first black graduate of West Point.

The Despoilers (Five Star Westerns, 2002) and *Ghost Legion* (Five Star Westerns, 2005) are set in the Carolina backcountry during the Revolutionary War. *The Big Fifty* (Five Star Westerns, 2003) chronicles the slaughter of buffalo on the southern plains in the 1870s, while *East of the Border* (Five Star Westerns, 2004) is a comedy about the theatrical offerings of Buffalo Bill Cody, Wild Bill Hickok, and Texas Jack Omohundro, and *Camp Ford* (Five Star Westerns, 2005) tells about a Civil War baseball game between Union prisoners of war and Confederate guards. "Boggs' narrative voice captures the old-fashioned style of the past," *Publishers Weekly* said, and *Booklist* called him "among the best Western writers at work today." Boggs lives with his wife Lisa and son Jack in Santa Fe. His website is www.JohnnyDBoggs.com. His next Five Star Western will be *Greasy Grass*.